INCUBATE

a horror collection of feminine power

Edited by

LCW Allingham

River Eno and Susan Tulio

To Elizabeth, to Malala, to Gloria and Roxane.
To women who push forward when no one else
can. To Sacheen and Marsha, to Ruth, Grace and
Bell. To our grandmothers and mothers and
to all of us as well.

CONTENTS

Foreword   vii

Ef Deal

The New Wife   I

A.R.C. Mitra

Aggrieved   27

Hope Madden

The Dogs   43

Maureen O'Leary

The Town Bike   59

LCW Allingham

Motherhood Changes You   79

Dale W. Glaser

A Hole Where Your Back Should Be   117

Sofia Tantono

Perfect Immortality   133

River Eno

Famine   147

Sydney Hodges

Acknowledgements   157

Author Bios   161

FOREWORD

What does *The Jetsons* have in common with the *U.S.S Enterprise*, Garman, Siri, and Alexa?

Set that aside for the moment while I tell a tale.

I was born into a Catholic family, raised in Catholic schools, and by the time I was eight I knew exactly what I wanted to be in life: a martyr.

Every First Friday of the month, we kids got trooped into the church for the Mass; for, as we were taught, if you attended the Mass every First Friday, you got to go to heaven. After the Mass, we gathered in the assembly hall for an inspirational movie. *Song of Bernadette, Joan of Arc, The Miracle of Marcelino, The Robe*—wonderful, bloody tales of young people being abused, tortured, debased, slaughtered, and going to heaven for all their pains. And oh, the Christmas story! When the angel Gabriel told Mary God was going to impregnate her, she said, "My soul magnifies the Lord, my spirit rejoices in God my Savior, for he has looked with favor on this lowly handmaiden...May it be done to me according to your word."

There it is in a nutshell.

I came to believe being a submissive victim of sexual assault was a sure road to martyrdom and heaven. So, when I was shoved into a closet every week for four years to be molested by a universally revered man, I figured I was suffering my way to heaven. I didn't like it. I knew something was off. I was ashamed and I felt filthy, but I believed I deserved it somehow, and all this was meant to happen so I could glorify God and go to heaven. But as I grew older, I began to doubt how allowing someone else to commit sins using my body would get my soul to heaven. When I asked a priest about it, he told me if I questioned the will of God, I should get out of the church. So, being the obedient Catholic, I got out.

In the many years since, I've grown a lot wiser about my situation, and I've come to acknowledge a few important facts:

1) I didn't deserve it.

2) The old man was a son of a bitch and everyone knew it, but no one wanted to topple the statue.

3) There is a roiling miasma of vitriolic, toxic, and utterly justified rage inside me that demands a reckoning that will never come, and every day I see the scales tip further and

further to the side that seeks to systematically abuse, torture, debase, and slaughter women.

4) I'm not alone in that rage.

And don't you dare tell me it's just my time of the month.

In 1972, while I was still struggling with awareness of my new self, Alice Paul came to speak at my college. Alice Paul began her struggle to obtain equal status for women under the law in 1907, and relentlessly fought a sixty-seven-year crusade for an official amendment to the Constitution, the Equal Rights Amendment, a statement that seems so obvious, so simple in a country that pledges liberty and justice for all: *"Men and women shall have equal rights throughout the United States and every place subject to its jurisdiction."* She began with suffrage and enfranchisement in 1907, moved to labor status, and eventually to issues of autonomy; e.g., the right to a credit card, the right to purchase a car or house on loan, the right to have one's Fallopian tubes tied without a spouse's or parent's consent, or the right to choose not to carry a fetus to term when impregnated. For those basic rights, Alice Paul endured abuse and torture from the media, politicians, law enforcement, and even fellow suffragists. If you are reading this and don't know her story, go do your research. If the nuns had taught us *that* story, we might be living in a different world today.

Fifty years on, we have women on the Supreme Court, in the White House, in the Senate, and in Congress, but women have yet to gain the equal status with men Alice Paul so aggressively sought—or that any woman who knows the difference between right and wrong instinctively seeks. Bit by bit, women have lost ground due to the corruption of political standards, and women are expected to accept their appointed role of "lowly handmaiden."

The 2022 decision of the Supreme Court in *Dobbs v. Jackson Women's Health Organization* to overturn the precedent set by *Roe v. Wade* in 1973 removed all federal protection of a woman's right to abort an unwanted or non-viable fetus. The basis of this decision was purely political and utterly unconstitutional in nature, using a single religion's unscientific view that life begins at conception, to justify granting a fetus the right to life. Ironically, many states quickly adopted abortion laws that deny the right to life for the mother, criminalizing miscarriages and abruptions, and forbidding abortion in situations, such as ectopic pregnancies, which threaten the mother's life. Already we have seen a ten-year-old girl traveling to another state to obtain the abortion of a pregnancy that was the result of a rape. The girl was told by her own state officials that her fetus was a gift from God, a blessing.

Meanwhile, year by year, we watch rapists freed from prison without serving full sentences. All-star athlete, Brock Turner, raped an unconscious woman three times, and he served all of three months. We see defense attorneys accuse young women who press charges against their rapists of "deserving," "asking for," and "soliciting" the rape. Almost one million rapes or sexual assaults were reported in 2019, and officials acknowledge that less than 20% of rapes that occur are reported to authorities. If you can't do the math, I can spell it out: Men commit an estimated five million rapes or sexual assaults each year. Moreover, 82% of those rapes are against girls between the ages of fourteen and seventeen. Hundreds of thousands of rape kits go unlogged or investigated, and are eventually invalidated altogether.

The disparity between the sexes covers most of daily life. Women earn eighty-two cents to a man's dollar in salaries. Although women hold 52% of managerial posts, men outnumber women seventeen to one at the CEO level. Men are more likely to be murdered (76.8%), but of the other 23.2% of murder victims, (*i.e.,* women) 63.7% are victims of domestic homicides and 81.7 % are victims of sex-related homicides. 50.5% of the US population is female, but female representation in Congress is only 27%, and let's face it, that includes Marjorie Taylor Greene and Lauren Boebert. Enough said.

Have you solved the riddle yet? It's this:

In 1962, Jane and George Jetson enjoyed the housemaid services of Rosie the Robot. Four years later, the starship *Enterprise* appeared, representing a 20th-century vision of diverse 23rd-24th centuries, where the ship's computer can locate anyone on the ship, identify intruders, direct you to the bar, provide an entertaining holographic environment, cook you a meal, and serve you "Tea. Earl Grey. Hot." Garman GPS was introduced in 1989, ready to guide you anywhere in the world without having to consult a paper map. Siri, Apple iPhone's personal assistant introduced in 2011, could get you all the information you needed at hand, and even dial your phone for you. Alexa in 2013 became Amazon's fly-on-the-wall source of information and full access to entertainment and shopping.

In every one of these assistant devices, the default voice is female—all-wise, all-knowing, and utterly subservient.

Like A.R.C. Mitra's Shanice, once married to a gaslighting son-of-a-bitch. Like LCW Allingham's quartet of girls forced to endure lessons on how to be good girls while Samantha lay dead on the rocks. Like Dale Glaser's Nicola, whose true identity was lost in her assigned, contractual role as SAHM. Like Sofia Tantono's Ayu, the victim of rape and pedophilia. Like River Eno's bride, never perfect enough for her husband.

I believe Sydney Hodges' "Famine" best explains the misogyny that has kept women in the role of the ship's computer, the electronic assistant, the eternal lesser-than: "The world has always feared what doesn't serve it...They never wanted the richness within you, only what you could do for them."

The authors whose works you will read in these pages feel the rage I feel and have felt for most of my life. This is not an anthology of hatred against men; it's a collective representation of a systematic prison, from a generation fed up with constraints placed upon women as human beings, deemed incapable of handling any position of authority, especially the responsibility of making decisions about their own health and welfare and their role in society, a restriction no man in America has to endure.

It's wrong. *It has always been wrong.*

Woe betide when that roiling miasma gives birth to the creature incubating within.

-Ef Deal, author of *Esprit de Corpse*
2022

INCUBATE

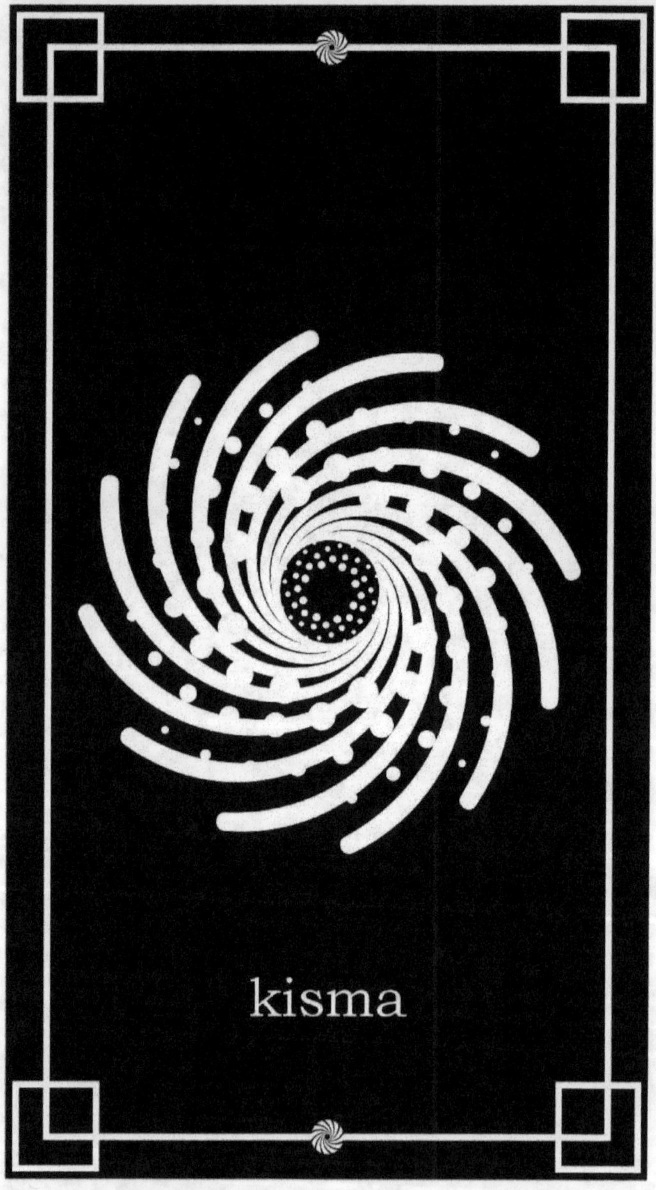

kisma

The New Wife

A.R.C. Mitra

She *was* pretty. Exactly his type—tall, skinny, smooth ebony skin, big dark eyes, hair bunched up on the top of her head in a deliberately messy way, as if to say, *I don't really care.* Obviously, she did. Girl probably spent hours in front of the mirror teasing those curls so that they sprung out in just the right way. I'd stand across the street from the house – *my* house – and watch her go for a run at the crack of dawn each day, in designer yoga pants and a teeny-tiny sports bra, her washboard flat stomach on full display. *Of course* she was the type of woman who would wake up at 4 a.m. to go for a run.

After her run, she'd go back inside the house, only to emerge again an hour or so later wearing a perfectly pressed pencil skirt and starched white shirt, glossy leather handbag dangling from the crook of her arm. She would slide gracefully into her cute little car, one sleek high-heeled leg after the other. What was she, a lawyer? A banker? Peter always did like his women smart, just not smart enough to figure him out.

I watched the house every day. What else did I have to do? I would usually hang around across the street, but sometimes I got closer and peered through the bay window at the front. I used to sit by that window and work, back when it was my house. My brain hurt to think of it, a corrosive, bitter pain, like someone had opened the top of my skull and poured acid into it.

They never saw me watching them, even though I saw them. They actually seemed happy. Sometimes I would see her, the new wife, sitting on the couch, and he would bring her a cup of coffee or a glass of wine, and she would look up at him with a gleaming smile. I would remember how once upon a time, I was happy too. As I watched them, rage would wash over me, a rage so all-consuming that it could swallow all three of us—Peter, the new wife, and me—whole.

Sometimes, I thought of burning the house down with them in it. Why should Peter have it all, when I was banished out in the cold?

Other times, I was more clear-headed about the whole thing. I had looked a lot like the new wife, once. Menopause had done away with *my* flat stomach and *my* wild black curls had started going grey. It was little surprise that Peter had decided to trade me in for a younger model. Besides, as I had realized too late, Peter had other reasons for getting rid of me.

There were no two ways about it, the new wife was gorgeous. Too bad she was going to die soon.

✳

I tried following the new wife to work; tried getting a better idea of what she did all day, but I kept losing her at the end of the street. So, one morning, after both she and Peter had left for work (after an obligatory kiss in the driveway to make the neighbors jealous) I decided to check out the house instead. It was absurdly easy for me to get in.

It was the first time I had been inside the house since I left, since Peter *made* me leave. They had erased all traces of me already. It hurt more than I expected to see her face cream, her clock, and her book on my bedside table; to see her clothes hanging on my side of the closet. Worst of all, when I opened the jewelry box on the dressing table, I saw my earrings inside. Peter must have given them to her. I wondered if she knew they had belonged to me, and if so, if it gave her the creeps. I wondered if any of the jewelry Peter had given me had ever belonged to someone else.

It was so easy to get into the house that I began snooping around frequently when Peter and the new wife were out. At first, I would just wander around, marveling at all the things that had changed. But one day, I went inside with a greater sense of purpose. I simply could not allow Peter and the new wife to live in that house as if I had never been there, as if I had never existed. That day, I smashed a bunch of wine glasses on the kitchen floor, emptied all the cereal boxes onto the living room carpet and pulled all the drawers out of the bedroom dressers. Childish, I know, but it was therapeutic.

After I did all that, I took a minute to think about things, and an idea came to me. A better idea than simply destroying the house. I went to the master bedroom ensuite. The double vanity was just as I remembered, and a vivid image of Peter and me standing side by side, brushing our teeth, flashed before my eyes. Except now, on what had been my side, all *her* cosmetics were lined up. I ran my fingers across the array of expensive products (did *anyone* need that many eye creams?) and selected a golden tube of lipstick. I took the lid off and twisted the bottom. A burgundy stick emerged. I'd worn a shade very much like that, once upon a time.

I leaned over and began to write across the mirror with the lipstick, in capital letters as large as I could manage. I'd been wanting to do that ever since I saw Elizabeth Taylor do it in a movie. When I was finished, I dropped the ruined lipstick and stepped back to admire my handiwork.

GET OUT, OR YOU'LL DIE.

It was the first thing I'd written in a long time, and I was pretty happy with how it turned out.

I left the house after that, assumed my usual vantage point across the street and waited for the new wife. She always came home before Peter, so that she could cook dinner and then spend a few more hours working, often late into the night. I'd seen it all, through their windows.

She got home that day just after 6 p.m., as usual. I watched her get out of her car, tote bag swinging from one arm and files tucked under the other, not breaking a sweat as she trotted up to the front door in four-inch stilettos and a skintight skirt. She went inside, and as she did so, I got a little distracted thinking about how great her butt looked in that skirt. Soon enough, she rushed back outside, now looking slightly disheveled. She began pacing back and forth on the front lawn, talking animatedly into a cell phone. I couldn't hear her clearly over the sound of evening traffic from the nearby highway, but it was obvious that she was speaking to Peter, because eventually she tossed the phone onto the grass, stopped pacing and pressed the palm of one hand against her forehead. I knew *that* feeling. Peter used to give me a headache too.

I knew, also, how the conversation must have gone. She would have told Peter that someone had broken into the house, and he would have scolded her for being hysterical. It was probably the first taste the new wife had ever had of what Peter was really like.

She stood there for a while, running her fingers through her hair. Her messy-not-messy hairstyle devolved into decidedly messy territory. She kicked off her stilettos and began pacing across the lawn again in her stocking feet.

Peter finally arrived, and he and the new wife spoke outside. He grabbed her elbow and tried to pull her inside, but she flung her arm away from him and spoke rapidly, waving her hands around as she did so. I caught snatches of what she said: *someone's broken in, someone's threatening me.* I wasn't really listening. I was staring at Peter. It had been a while since I had seen him so clearly. He was handsome as ever, and even from where I stood, I could see that brilliant flash of white teeth as he gave the new wife his old reassuring smile, the one he had given me a thousand times. And—I could hardly believe it—he was wearing the coat I had given him on our last anniversary. Discarded the wife, kept the coat. I had to look away. Something inside me ached, looking at him. It was surprising. I didn't know I was capable of still feeling like that.

When I looked back, Peter and the new wife had gone inside. A little while later, the police arrived. I didn't care. They'd never know it was me.

The next day, a couple of men showed up in a large van and spent hours installing lights and cameras all around the exterior of the house and, presumably, inside too. I watched with mild amusement. Thanks to Peter, I could evade those cameras easily. If they thought a security system was going to keep me out, they had another thing coming.

I left Peter and the new wife alone for a few days after that, long enough for them to sink back into a false sense of security. Then I went inside the house again when they were out, and this time my activities inside were not so childish. I pulled a knife out of the block on the kitchen counter—he'd renovated the entire kitchen since he got rid of me; the new wife was enjoying the granite countertop I had always wanted—went upstairs and slashed their bedsheets into ribbons. I opened their closets and did likewise to his clothes. He was dressing better these days too, I noted, as I sliced through a couple of linen jackets. I guess that's what coming into money does for you. When I was done with his clothes, I turned to hers. I was a little nicer to her. I left the silk slip dress and the cashmere sweaters intact.

I went over to his study and pulled his precious books off the shelves, for good measure. After that, I rifled through the papers stacked atop his desk. Most of them were innocuous, but I read them anyway, out of idle curiosity, and eventually I got to the good stuff. It looked like he owed a lot of people a lot of money, and I was pretty sure I knew why. It took me a lot of thinking, after it was over between me and Peter, but I ultimately concluded that he had a spending problem, and probably a gambling problem, and was likely embezzling funds from his psychiatry practice to boot. To think that he used to tell me *I* had problems.

I was surprised, though, to see debts mounting up again so soon. I had expected that the money he got after I was gone had fixed everything for him. It was such a lot of money, after all. But Peter, as I had discovered too late, probably couldn't help himself. He always had to have something better, something more.

I swept the papers off his desk, watched them float haphazardly down to the floor, and sat in his chair for a while. For a moment, I contemplated staying there and letting him see me when he got home, then decided against it, and instead dug around in the desk drawers until I found a black marker pen. I went back down to the living room, pressed the tip of the marker to a wall and began to write, as gleefully as a child, in big looping cursive, all across the freshly painted walls: *Get out, or you'll die. Leave him, or you'll die.* I could have been more explicit, but I figured I'd save it for next time.

The police came again that night. I saw it all from across the street. They must have reviewed the footage from those fancy security cameras and seen nothing. The next morning, I watched Peter install yet more lights in the front yard and a few more cameras. That afternoon, someone came and changed all the locks. It didn't matter. I would keep coming, and they wouldn't see me. Not unless I wanted them to.

The next time I went inside the house, I left the taps running and flooded all the bathrooms. I watched the water pool over the new marble tiles and remembered how much *I* had wanted marble floors. Peter always told me they were too expensive. I smashed a couple of windows. I ran all of Peter's papers through the shredder.

I kept it up over the next few months, different variations of destruction. Every time, I left messages for her, scrawled on the walls and mirrors and on the pages of the books on her bedside table: *Leave him, or you'll die.*

My activities were taking a toll on the new wife. She always looked anxious now, and when she went for her morning run, she would glance over her shoulder at regular intervals. After a while, she stopped running altogether, and started going to work later and later. When she finally went out each day, her clothes were rumpled, her hair pulled back severely with no real attempt to style it, and she had swapped the stilettos for flats. Upon arriving home in the evenings, she would pause before unlocking the front door and take a lipstick-sized tube of pepper spray out of her bag before going inside. On the days that I had been in the house, she'd invariably run back outside seconds after going in, yelling into her cell phone. Sooner or later, Peter would show up to placate her and convince her to go back into the house. On one such occasion, after they went inside I snuck into the garden and listened to them talking through an open window.

"I just don't understand it, Peter," the new wife was saying. "Every time, the security footage is just blank. It just cuts out."

"I don't know what you want me to say," Peter said, in that tensely reasonable tone I knew all too well. "We've tried three different companies now. We've spent tens of thousands of dollars."

"It has to be someone you know," she said. "The messages...are you sure it's not some woman?"

"How many times have I told you, there is no woman," Peter said. I could hear the threat of anger rumbling in his throat.

"Do you know anyone who can tamper with the cameras?" the new wife asked, undeterred.

"Look, I know you've been under a lot of stress at work," Peter said. "Have you ever had..." He paused, as though searching for the correct word, "*episodes* before, where you're missing time?"

There was a long silence.

"What exactly are you trying to say?"

"I had a patient once," Peter said. "Who, when under stress, would forget doing things."

Ah. This too was familiar. Peter the psychiatrist, psychoanalyzing his wife.

"You—you think—you actually think *I'm* doing this? Oh my god. Oh my god, Peter."

I peeked through the window and saw the new wife backing away from Peter, her hands covering her face.

"Honey, you *do know* how to operate the cameras."

"I can't believe you would say that. I just can't believe it."

The new wife stormed out of the room, and a door slammed shut somewhere in the distance. I couldn't help smiling. Maybe it was working. Peter would drive the new wife away, all by himself. And then I could have Peter, all to myself.

✳

Peter must really have gotten his hooks into the new wife, because she stuck around. In fact, she started working from home, at his suggestion. I heard him tell her that he doubted the person responsible would try anything if someone was at home. At first, she balked at the idea, arguing that it would make her a sitting duck, but he wore her down, as I knew he would. For the first week or so, she put on an impossibly white T-shirt and impossibly tight jeans, sat at the dining table and worked steadily on her laptop, speaking authoritatively on conference calls. Then she got into the habit of pouring herself a large glass of wine in the afternoons, and soon enough she was refilling that glass too many times to be doing any real work. I peeked through the dining room window and watched her as she loafed around in an oversized sweatshirt and pajama pants. Still annoyingly cute, but not quite the Amazonian beauty she used to be.

I thought it might work out after all. Peter might lose interest now that the new wife had lost some of her glamour. I'd forgotten, though, that Peter liked his women a little depressed, a little cut off from the world. All I had done was make things easier for him.

I decided it was time to amp things up some more.

I started sneaking into the house while she was home. I kept it subtle at first. No more breaking things or writing on the walls and mirrors. I would just move things, hide them. Just enough to freak her out a little bit. I put her wallet in the pantry and her car keys in her face cream. I hid her jewelry box under Peter's desk and her bedroom slippers in the garage. On a few occasions, I slammed some doors. She began searching the entire house at regular intervals during the day, armed with a kitchen knife and pepper spray, but she never saw me.

I heard them fighting more often now. She had started insisting that they move, and he steadfastly refused. He was an idiot. It would have been in his best interests to move too. Surely it could not have escaped him that the person who was breaking into the house was after him too; knew his secrets. But he didn't seem to care. Peter's ego, his belief that things would always go his way, astounded me. Why shouldn't he be arrogant? Things *had* always gone his way.

Then, he *really* started accusing her of doing it all herself. I was surprised to find that I derived no satisfaction watching her begging him to believe her. Again, I hoped that the new wife would decide to leave on her own, but still she stayed with him, in that house.

One day, while she was in the bathroom, I typed her a note on her laptop: *"If you want it to stop, leave him."*

When she came back, she sat down at the dining table and stared at the note for a long time. Then she put her face in her hands and began to cry.

Jeez. Had Peter really convinced her that she *was* crazy?

A week later, she went out for the first time in a while. Judging by her clothes—a baggy t-shirt and leggings that she'd been wearing for the past three days—it was nowhere special. Probably the grocery store, to replenish her stock of junk food; lately she'd replaced wine with tubs of ice cream and bars of chocolate. That flat stomach wouldn't last long at this rate.

I took the opportunity of having the house to myself to trash the master bedroom again. When I emptied the garbage bin in the ensuite bathroom onto the floor, I discovered why she'd ditched the wine. Amidst the empty toilet rolls and crumpled tissues that tumbled out of the bin was a pregnancy test. It was of the type you always saw advertised on TV these days; no messing around with one line or two with these ones, just the word neatly spelled out in little black letters: *Pregnant.*

Well. That was unexpected. They'd been married for like, two seconds.

I had no choice after that. That pregnancy test forced my hand.

＊

She went out again a couple of days later, this time probably for a meeting. She was dressed in office clothes, although her blouse was creased, and her jacket was a different shade of blue than her skirt. While she was out, I slipped inside the house again. I knew it was time to really spell it out for her. I went up to the ensuite bathroom, back to the vanity that had once been mine, once again took one of her lipsticks and wrote across the mirror the words I had not been able to bring myself to write before: *Leave him, or he'll kill you.*

It was even harder to write than I had expected. Writing it made it real. I forced myself to write three more words, the most painful of them all.

He killed me.

I sat down in the corner of the bedroom, on the little velvet stool I had once lovingly chosen, and I waited.

＊

She was only gone for a few hours. I heard her unlock the front door and come upstairs. She entered the bedroom and from my spot in the corner, I saw her kick off her shoes and toss her handbag onto the bed. She didn't see me. I had learned some time ago that my default state these days was invisible, and in any case, I wanted her to see the message before she saw me. I watched her go into the bathroom and then I heard a little yelp of shock. She rushed back out of the bathroom, retrieved her phone from her handbag and made a call.

"Peter, you have to come home. It's happened again!"

Oh god. Was this girl an idiot? I literally spelled it out for her, and she went and called Peter. There's really only so much you can do.

I listened to the rest of the call with mounting impatience. Peter, it appeared, was out of town and would not be home that night. She hung up the phone and thudded downstairs. I heard her rushing around the house, flinging open doors, likely doing her usual routine with the knife and pepper spray. Then she came back upstairs and flung herself onto the bed, sobbing. I watched her for a while. If she thought she had things to cry about now, she didn't know what was coming.

Finally, she sat up. Dusk had fallen, and the light was quickly fading. She wiped her eyes, and I decided that was a good time to let her see me. I wasn't quite sure if it would work, but I concentrated hard.

From her reaction I knew that she saw me.

She screamed, of course. I knew what I must look like. There's a dent in the side of my head from falling down the stairs.

A dent in the side of my head, matted with hair and blood, from falling down the stairs, after Peter pushed me.

And from the hammer.

In addition to the dent, my left arm was at a weird angle, because it broke when I fell, and I was missing a lot of teeth. In the movies, when people die after falling down the stairs, they look like they're sleeping. In real life, if the fall is bad enough, it really messes you up. Peter knew that. Peter knew it would mess me up bad enough to kill me. Well, almost kill me. The hammer finished the job.

"What do you want?" the new wife gasped, when she had finished screaming.

I couldn't see her too clearly in the darkening room, mainly just the outline of her body and the whites of her terrified round eyes, but it seemed she could see me just fine.

"I want you to leave Peter," I said simply. "You must know who I am."

"No," she whispered. "No, I don't know."

"Didn't you feel weird moving into the house where Peter's previous wife died?"

Realization, comprehension, flooded that pair of beautiful eyes, glistening in the darkness.

"You're Shanice," she said. It had been such a long time since anyone had said my name. "I'm sorry. It was a terrible accident."

She really did sound sorry. The new wife was probably an ok person.

"Peter's wives have a lot of accidents," I said softly. "The one before me died in a terrible accident too, you know. Skiing. Her face was a mess too." I paused, to let it sink in. "Oh honey, how do you think Peter got you those marble floors and that nice granite countertop?"

I heard her swallow, but she said nothing.

"I bet you have a great career," I said. "Lawyer?"

"Stockbroker," she said hoarsely.

"Professor. Head of the Faculty of History, actually," I said, touching my chest with my good hand. "Professionals get insured for a lot, you know.

The one before me was an architect. Bet you have a good policy too, huh? You have no idea just how much financial trouble Peter is in, do you? Don't feel bad. I didn't either."

"Peter wouldn't..." she started to say, but she trailed off, because there I was, the inconvertible evidence. I moved closer to her, and I reached out and touched her cheek. My hand must have been very cold because she winced but, to my surprise, she did not pull away.

And just like that, she wasn't the new wife anymore. She was Alexis, a stockbroker who loved herself enough not to force her wild curls into a perm, who enjoyed running, who had a weakness for white wine and gorgeous shoes, who wore pajama pants with kittens printed on them when she worked from home. Just as I had become real to her, she had become real to me.

"Oh honey," I said. "You have a nice face. Don't let him mess it up."

✳

If I'd just had a woman-to-woman chat with Alexis in the beginning, I probably could have saved us both a lot of trouble. It was the pregnancy that convinced me to make myself visible to her; there was no way Peter would want a kid around when he was planning on getting rid of her. Once he found out she was pregnant, he would finish her off quickly.

She packed up her bags quickly after we had our conversation and got out of there. I hung around. I thought it would be enough to get her to leave Peter, but it wasn't enough. So, I waited all through the night for Peter to come home. I would have waited longer than that. I had time.

It was morning when I heard the front door open. I heard Peter walking around downstairs, calling her name, and then the sound of his footsteps on the staircase. He came into the room, and the briefcase tumbled from his hand and fell open, sending papers flying across the floor. He gaped at me, mouth hanging open, as I stood there in the sunlight streaming through the window, a ray of warmth I could not feel.

I had never seen Peter look scared, or at a loss for words. There's a first time for everything.

He said, at last, "You're not real. You can't...be real."

"I am," I said simply. God damn it, Peter was *not* going to gaslight me about my own death.

I concentrated harder. I could *feel* myself become more substantial. Something warm and wet trickled down the side of my head and dripped onto the floor, and I knew it was blood.

Peter blinked several times in rapid succession, as though hoping that I would disappear. When I didn't, he spoke again.

"What did you do with her? What have you done to her?"

"She's gone," I said quietly. "Did you think I'd let you get away with it? Did you think I'd let you do it again?"

"It was an accident," Peter said, his voice strangled despite his obvious efforts to remain calm.

"You threw me down the stairs," I said, advancing on him. "You think I don't remember? I remember everything. I remember you standing over me at the bottom of the staircase, waiting for me to stop breathing."

I *did* remember it all. I remembered lying there, trying more than anything to survive. I remembered how he got impatient, how I didn't die soon enough. How he got a hammer to finish the job. I remembered that final blow.

There was silence, other than the *drip drip drip* of my blood falling onto the floor, the hardwood floor I had once been so excited to put in. I moved closer to him.

"Do you know what it feels like, when someone bashes half your head in?"

Peter said nothing. He didn't really have to. He would know himself, soon enough.

❋

That fancy winding staircase was very *Gone With the Wind*, but it was a hazard. That's what the police said to Peter in the days after my death. Those were the days when I was still floating along, carried by the wind, and I drifted by the open window while the officers sat in the living room with Peter.

It wasn't a surprise that Peter should fall down those stairs too. He didn't die right away either. It must have been excruciating, lying there at the base of the stairs in the empty house, hoping his wife, his new wife, would come home and find him, blood turning his graying blonde hair crimson. It was just bad luck that Alexis wasn't there, the neighbors said; they had seen her leave, suitcase in hand, the evening before he got home.

The neighbors must have talked about it for weeks afterwards. But I didn't stick around to listen in on all their conversations, not this time. I moved on a week or so after Peter died. Left this earthly realm, you might say.

I could have gone earlier, but I chose to stay, to take care of the Peter situation. Why did I go through all that trouble, you ask? Well, to be honest, I was pretty pissed off about what Peter did to me. Anyway, I couldn't let it happen to another woman. Call me a feminist, I guess.

rāham

Aggrieved

Hope Madden

"You do not age."

It's as much a complaint as a compliment coming from Michael Palmiotto, Freshman Comp, who laughs when he says it. Michael laughs when he says most things.

"Blood of virgins," she answers. "You look glorious, by the way—sort of sun kissed."

"Oh!" Another giggle. "We just got back from Cape Coral. It was a family thing, but we did steal away for an afternoon alone here and there."

Michael and she stand bantering at Sopron College's annual *Shit, It's That Time Again* bash, thrown by Anthony and Sande Rahn the weekend before fall semester every year for at least sixteen or seventeen years. Buildings buzz with fluorescent lighting and anxious students, and the non-tenure-track gather in the Rahn back yard, within the comforting circle of stringed lights and tiki torches.

"Missed you the last couple of these." A wet salsa stain almost hides in the red floral pattern of Michael's Hawaiian shirt. "Where have you been?"

"I've actually been doing high school."

Michael looks surprised—kind of a cross between intrigued and aghast.

"I know." She laughs. "But there was a need for more counselors, and it felt—" She pauses, thinking of the right word, the word that would not read as pretentious or self-aggrandizing. "—compelling."

"How did it pay?"

"Comparably, honestly. But the hours are more draining, and the act of training children to deal with an active shooter..."

"Soul crushing." No giggle this time. "Let's grab one of those slushy margaritas and numb ourselves."

They meander to a festive table—two long conference tables the Rahns "borrowed" from school 16 years ago—skirted with parrots clutching lime slices in their beaks.

"We had our own issue, obviously..." Michael half-whispers. "I mean, we all should have seen it coming. That Evan Connors was Satan in expensive sneakers. Is that why you came back?"

"I did hear, of course. But no. I've grown weary of active shooters. I'm just here for Intro Soc and Social Problems." She points. "Is that Paul?"

Michael looks, squints.

"I haven't seen him since the before times." She points again to a shadowy back corner of the yard and turns to Michael. "Be right back."

She wanders toward the underlit bits of the yard, sneaks to the gate, ducks out of sight. The air is damp. The scent is dirty and old. She takes it in and moves, not quickly but with purpose, through campus and toward town.

She passes the dive bar, Varsity Club, already crowding with new and returning students. She eyes the youngsters—bright lips, tanned skin, processed hair—collecting outside to smoke, but walks on.

She passes the street corner that marks the end of Odenton's downtown, crosses the bridge over the brown water of the Euclid, and meanders toward the overly large and unkempt houses of the neighborhoods.

She crosses the street and looks through the smeared glass and into the garishly lit Lawson's convenience store.

Brian is working. He has a triangular face — wide set eyes and a pointy chin. He's scraping something crusty with his fingernail from his brown and orange smock and startles at the jangle of the bells hanging from the door.

※

Jesus, her again. Six nights in a row! She's a goddamn stalker. At least she's not in front of his house this time.

She drifts up and down aisles, her fingers trailing across overpriced canned goods, jerky, donuts. She pulls a Green Monster energy drink from a cooler and pivots toward Brian, smiling. Instead of setting the can on the counter, she hands it to him. Grimacing, he turns the wet can so he can scan it and sets it on the counter.

There is a pause. He looks at her. His eyes dart toward the purchase price written right there on the register display, then roll back toward her. She smiles serenely at him and waits.

"Dollar ninety-nine," Brian sighs. He looks, not at her face but at the chip display just over her right shoulder.

"Is this flavor any good?"

"Yeah, it's fine." *Why in the fuck ask me? What does she need, a curated beverage list?*

She smiles. She reaches into her pants pocket and hands him two singles. They are warm.

She waits for the penny back, almost smiling.

She opens the can and takes a big, open-mouthed drink, winces a little and smiles again. Has she been looking at him this whole time?

"Thanks, Brian."

He frowns when he hears his name, even though it's right there on his yellowing nametag.

She leaves.

He pulls his backpack out from under the counter. Careful not to jostle anything, he nabs a notebook.

She came again. Pocket money. Curated drink list? I. Would. Not. Drink. This. Piss.

He pulls out his phone and texts Owen.

Dude this woman was just in here

He leans on the counter and waits. His phone says 10:20, time to add milk to the shake machine. He stands, pulls a thick yellowish plastic bag of soft serve base from the reach-in cooler. Yanking the plastic ring and attaching the lip to the machine, he fondles the full, smooth bag and squeezes, hard, hard, hard, pushing the milky sweet concoction in a rush into the machine. The machine belches it back a bit. He sighs, reaches for a stiffening white towel, wipes up the mess, tips the bag to get the rest of the contents into the machine, wipes again, and throws both the towel and spent plastic bag into the trash.

His phone dings and he picks it up.

Was she hot?

Brian sighs.

She was old

He thinks about it, deletes.

Kinda

He stares again at the chips that were behind her shoulder. He struggles to picture her. How old was she? Was she old?

He deletes again.

Yeah but stupid

Pause.

Had to explain that she would have to in fact pay for that energy drink before she could leave the store thank you so much fucking idiot cunt

He waits.

Woa man take it easy sounds like a bitch tho lmao

Brian holds an angry breath. Owen is an idiot. Evan would have had this whole rant ready. Evan could always pinpoint exactly the type of bitch, and had these perfect names for them. Brian could never do that, label them right. And Owen was useless. But even talking about Evan now got people all unnerved. Forget about posting. That's what fucked Evan. The minute he shouted "Skank City" everybody knew who he was and which sorority was next because of that one post. Posts ruin you, even if you delete them. Let the cops find Brian's notebook. After the deed is done. Old school.

Metal jingle at the door. Gunther. Late Shift Gunther.

That's what his name tag says: Late Shift Gunther.

"Dude my dude!"

"Hey, Gunther. What's up?"

"I've mostly just been napping and staring. Oh, and I was playing this game with my neighbor?"

"That old lady?"

"Yeah, Miss Shan. There's this game we play for dollars called Screw Your Neighbor. She won like $4 off me tonight, and when I complained she told me I was butt-hurt."

Gunther laughs.

"Man, butt-hurt has got to be the word of the decade," Gunther muses. "Especially when an old lady says it. What about you, brother? Anything weird go down at our beloved L-Mart today?"

Brian thinks about mentioning her. Instead, he says, "No. But school starts tomorrow so you can probably expect some late, drunk college kids."

Gunther rests his bony ass against the counter. "College kids can fuck off."

Brian just hears it as the door jingle-bells shut behind him. He slips his notebook into his backpack, flat under the handgun wrapped in a towel, double straps, then mounts his bike and heads toward downtown.

Crossing the bridge, Brian thinks about how the air carries extra Euclid stink today, then realizes it's just the smell of the store blowing off his own clothes. He rolls to a stop at a four-way and looks toward the Varsity Club as a dirty white 4x4 crosses the intersection.

There she is. That's her, standing on the sidewalk in front of the bar. Does she see him? Is she staring at him? Dude, what is her problem?

He realizes he's been waiting, as if at a traffic light, instead of taking his immediate turn at the 4-way. Embarrassed, he fumbles to get the pedals moving and looks straight ahead as he passes, barely even hearing the meanness shouted at him from the bros and hos on the bar patio who recognize him.

＊

She watches. Her eyes track him from the bridge to the stop sign, then the next stop sign, on down Washington Street. She watches him until he and his bike are tiny, meaningless specks aimed at the dorms.

She steps onto Washington Street and walks—not slowly but not quickly, either—back toward campus.

She spies him, sitting on the wide concrete step of a closed print shop. The archway over the door and its shadow keep him hidden from the girls returning from Varsity Club to the house across the street. A sorority house. Naturally.

He's writing. His pack is open at his feet.

She stands bathed in the light from the streetlamp and waits. A long time passes. Brian looks across the street. Brian scribbles. Looks again. Finally, he turns his head and notices her in the light on the corner.

He looks like he's stopped breathing.

She crosses, catty corner, bisecting the intersection and moving directly toward him.

＊

What the fuck…

And then she just stands there. Not bossy, not anything, just standing, almost smiling. He stops writing. He presses his finger against his eyebrow and stares hard at the notebook. A car pulls in front of him, stops, and backs into the last, tight spot across the street. Girls spill out.

She's standing on the sidewalk, so obvious. They all look over.

She waves. She fucking waves!

"Everybody appreciates a good parallel parker," she calls. And then, to Brian, "Write that down in your book."

He shoves his notebook back into his pack.

"I'm not into MILFs."

Sly smile. "No?"

He doesn't say anything.

"I don't live here." What an idiotic thing to say! Like she's waiting for him to take her up to his room or something. Fuck!

"You don't live at the—which sorority house is this?" She points at the Tri Delta House.

"No, this place." He nods behind him at the empty print shop. It used to be Evan's mom's shop. There's an apartment upstairs that Evan had the keys to.

"No?"

He exhales angrily.

"Do you want to go for a walk?" she asks. "I live not too far that way."

She points back toward the faded commotion of downtown Odenton, Ohio.

He is frozen and blind and hot, not even sure if he's angry or embarrassed, they both bleed so easily one to the other. Before he realizes it, he's rushing past her. In a couple dozen steps or so he's back in his head and moving toward downtown.

He should have gone the other way, away from her place. No turning back now, she's probably still back there.

Fuck. The backpack.

"Forget something?"

"Jesus!" he starts. She's right behind him, almost close enough to whisper. She's holding his backpack. He grabs the pack and keeps moving forward, faster now. Fuck this bitch.

"You're lucky this is a small town," she calls to him. "A city of any size, there are security cameras everywhere." She's walking right next to him now. "You should be careful sitting at your not-apartment, you know? That's kind of what this college is known for now, right? Like the Kent State massacre, only instead of hippies and the National Guard it's sorority girls and an angry virgin?"

He stops. He's not sure if this feeling is fear or indignation or maybe protectiveness but it comes out as rage.

"What the fuck do you know about it?"

"Same as anybody else, news coverage and all. Spoiled white boy, young women minding their business, bullets instead of ejaculate." She leans in. "You don't want to be mistaken for the next entitled gunman, over there sketching pretty girls."

"I was writing!" And then again, more seething than yelling, "I was writing."

She grins. "I'd love to see your manifesto."

"Fuck you." He's walking again, still headed away from his bike. Evan had an Escalade.

Used, but still badass. Tinted windows. They sat higher than everyone except the townies with their monster truck tires.

"Where's your girlfriend?"

Is she making fun of him or flirting?

"Do you have one?"

"Yes."

"Then what are you doing sitting across from a sorority house eyeballing drunk girls as they come home?"

"I wasn't! Jesus! I was riding home, I had a thought, and I stopped to write it down."

Man, fuck this.

"Bitches, man," she says smiling.

He stops. "What do you want?"

She takes another long drag of night air. Ahead, streetlights brighten the waning nighttime bustle of downtown. But it's dark where they stand.

"I can't really have a college boy," she says.

He looks away from her.

"Frowned upon." She smiles. "But a boy from town I can have."

He turns his eyes back to her. She regards him with a sly smile and begins walking, slowly. Without really noticing, he follows.

"I'm not a boy."

"No. No, of course not. It's a relative thing. I'm new in town. I don't know anybody." She rolls her eyes. "I don't really want to know anybody."

What's going on?

"You don't seem to like knowing anybody, either," she says, as if it makes them symbiotic somehow.

"So why would I want to know you?"

She sighs. "I don't want you to know me. I just want you to come home with me."

She's stopped moving.

"Is this a joke?" He sneers it more than says it, but now he hopes it isn't a joke. He'd like to do it. Just get it over with. He wants to just do it and be done with it more than he wants her. Though she's not bad, but not—whatever, it's probably a joke.

"I'm right up there."

He turns and looks up at a bland brick building. She winks and nods toward the doorway behind him.

"I don't get it."

"I know you don't," she says, smirking. "I don't know you. You don't know me. I'm not exactly what you want but you are precisely what I am looking for."

She steps toward him, raises her hand, reaches for his hair. He flinches, almost imperceptibly. She stops, doesn't touch him. Instead, she slips past him, opens the door and takes the first step, calling behind her, "Do you want to come?"

He lets the door close. He notices again the weight of his backpack, lets it give him courage. He fondles the pack, finds the bulge of the towel and its loaded treasure and grins.

✳

She reopens the door.

"It's not usually this difficult," she smiles. He's not bad looking, honestly. It's so hard for the young to be ugly.

She pushes the door all the way open and waits. Patient.

Brian holds the backpack close in front of him. He laughs, an ugly laugh. Mean. He pushes past her and starts up the steps. She smiles more broadly and lets the door close behind her.

She won't even remember him, not really. Not cleanly. Not by name. Brian. God, isn't everyone named Brian? Delicious, sobbing, screaming Brian or Cameron or Seth, all of them saving themselves for her.

Damn, nothing tasted as good as self-righteous indignation and cowardice.

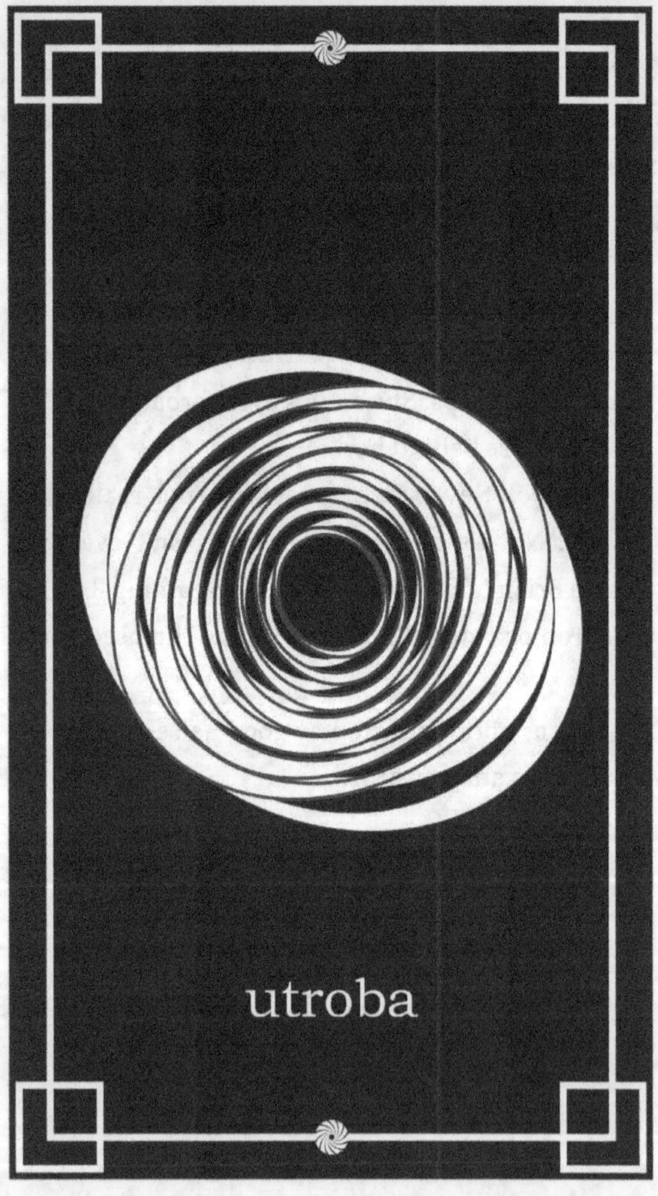
utroba

The Dogs

Maureen O'Leary

Cynthia didn't believe me that we needed to get through the Loomis Gap before sunset even though I insisted that we could not under any circumstances drive that part of Highway 39 after sundown.

We were in Queensville for a medical conference repping the drug company we worked for. My job was boring, but I was good at sales, and I loved money. Cynthia loved money too, but she wouldn't admit it. She wanted to be managing vice president, and managers didn't talk about loving money. They talked about *mission statements* and *quarterly reports*.

The sky turned a bad color of purple while Cynthia talked about dressing for the job you want, not the job you have. She wore restrictive underwear beneath her pencil skirts, which I knew because the company would only pay for one room at the conference, and so I was treated to the sight of Cynthia's behind squished into a tan-colored elastic operation every morning as she applied mascara.

She tapped the steering wheel with her pink acrylic fingernails. "More than one doctor at the luncheon assumed I was upper management. I mean, hello. Someday, right?"

The trees flew past in the half light. "What's the speed limit?" I asked. Whatever it was, she needed to go faster.

"You should know," she said. "You're the one who used to live up here."

There were no speed limit signs on this section of the highway because my old boyfriend and former friends kept removing them until finally the county gave up trying and let the region go all the way feral. I had posed the speed limit question to suggest she was going too slow in a nice way, because I didn't want to piss her off. She was my immediate supervisor, and I wanted her to like me, which is why I let her talk me into stopping for dinner at Applebee's even though the delay would land us on the highway through the Gap after nightfall.

"Take it from me," Cynthia was saying. "Find out whose job you want and start dressing better than that person. Get there earlier and leave later. Make sure your bosses know which sales are yours, and don't let anyone steal your thunder. I mean it, Casey. You have to stand up for yourself in this world."

"I really didn't want to be on this road at night," I said. There was a flash of movement in the shadows.

"Don't worry, I'm a great driver," she said just as a thunk under the wheels sent us spinning. As we spun I hoped that only one tire was wrecked. That maybe this was a mistake and not an intention. That maybe I could get the spare on quick enough to get us off the mountain safely.

The car slammed into a ditch and the airbags exploded in puffs of gunpowder. This was not an accident. The motorcycles were already upon us, a line of one-eyed headlights flooding the ruined car.

"What's happening?" Cynthia dabbed at her cheeks.

"You should have listened to me. That's what's happening," I said. The engines revved, echoing across the ravine so they sounded like hundreds and not just ten. Ten was enough. Ten was too many.

I climbed out on shaky legs. The engines cut out at once. "Goddamn, Casey. That you?" a familiar voice called from the other side of the beams.

"You know who it is." My chest ached at the unmistakable clink of the tire shredder getting pulled off the road. Victor swung his leg over his Harley, and the others yipped like puppies.

Glass crunched under Cynthia's heels as she limped to my side. She made a visor of her hand and peered into the lights. "Hello? Have you come to help us?"

The guys went quiet. Victor loped forward with his hands in his pockets. I locked my knees to hide their shaking. He tucked his chin as if daring me to be mad at him.

"Leave us alone, " I said.

"Too late for that, Queen."

I held my gaze. I could not look afraid. "I'm calling for a tow," I said.

"We're already here." He motioned to the side of the road and sure enough there was Boom leaning against the bumper of the Dog Boys Auto Repair tow truck.

"Boom can take us into town," I said, grasping at the last tissue-thin hope that Victor could be an adult man about my leaving him and let us go.

"Not an option," he said.

In the shadows the men shuffled their feet, their scent of sweat and leather rising in the cold air. They were already making me tired. I pinched the top of my nose and tried to think.

"I missed that," Victor said. There was good cheer in his voice. "You always used to do that when you were pissed at me."

"Let us go," I said.

"The thing is, you don't really want that. Because if you really wanted to leave then you would not have come through the Gap at night."

"That wasn't my fault," I said.

Cynthia raised a hand as if we were in school. "It was my fault. I didn't listen."

"Please stop talking, Cynthia," I said. Even in this trouble I hated telling my supervisor to shut up, but somebody had to.

Victor wore a fresh white t-shirt and the ends of his hair were wet from a shower. He was acting tough, but he'd dressed up for this. "You knew I would feel you coming through here," he said. "We are still connected, Casey."

"We also had a prospect stake out the Hilton in Queensville," Boom said. "We saw online that your company was sending reps to the conference and figured you might be local for a couple of days. But sure, Victor could *feel* you were coming." The guys laughed. Amos. Mister Pete. Maximo. All my old friends. My family.

Victor gave Boom the finger and ordered him to hitch Cynthia's car. A growl sounded from the shadows, and it was not an engine. It was an animal, and there was another. And another. I stepped back, pushing Cynthia behind me.

"What's happening?" she asked, and I couldn't answer. Her knowing what was happening wasn't going to help her survive. I was her only hope for that.

"Victor, I swear," I said. The cartilage in my ex-husband's nose crackled as his face lengthened into a snout. I started unbuttoning the polyester blouse I bought thinking I could pass it off for silk. As dumb as I took the guys for, I was the one caught in Loomis Gap with a cheap blouse and a trunk full of pharma samples. Maybe Victor was right. Maybe some part of me wanted him to catch me.

"Boom, take my friend to town and drop her off at a 7-eleven or something. She isn't part of this," I said. Boom looked at Victor for approval, and when he got the nod, he pulled Cynthia by her wrist to the truck's passenger side.

"Go," I said, my voice strange. My skirt puddled at my feet. Victor had already turned, nudging my hip with his nose, baring his teeth lightly against my skin. There was at least half a chance that Boom would take my direction and Cynthia would live through this. Boom was the gentlest one: the least likely to attack for no reason. She wasn't a threat. What would she say if she tried to call the police? *There were dogs, sir. Dogs on motorcycles. That is, at first they were really handsome men. I could see the appeal before my friend turned into a dog too and everything got out of hand.*

The truck rumbled down the highway as I ran through the woods. An owl's wings swished above my head, and Victor's breath was hot upon my neck. I made a wish for Cynthia to end the night under the cold fluorescent lights of a convenience store in the valley as I submitted to Victor under the moon.

✳

"Where you belong," Victor said as he followed me into the main house. I smelled other women there, but human women only. The ones the boys brought over sometimes to party. Victor didn't change another girl and neither did anyone else. I wasn't replaced.

I pulled pine needles from my hair. My lips felt swollen. Victor turned away, his broad back saying everything about his change of mood. "The guys are going to be hungry," he said.

My cheeks burned with shame. My welcome was over, and I was left in the filthy kitchen wondering what to make for dinner just like I never left. Victor was a hard man, and even though it was me who turned him the same as my mother turned my father and her mother before her turned my grandfather, I wasn't the one in charge. The women in my family turned our men and then couldn't escape them even when we tried.

I put on some of Maximo's clothes because he was the skinniest and the shortest. After cleaning the kitchen I found some chicken pieces in the freezer. They were probably taking turns cooking, God help them. I threw a pot of water on the stove to boil and hoped again that Boom left Cynthia alone as I threw together a meal that would please the pack of dogs I was responsible for making.

I made Victor when I was eighteen by biting him under the moonlight in the same clearing where my mother made my father. Then I broke the rules and bit Boomer too. Then Maximo and the rest. What can I say? I wanted a big family. Victor called us *The Dogs* and opened the repair shop as a front for running drugs through the Gap. It could be said that I abandoned my family when I left Victor the year before, thinking I could just choose to be free.

Boom returned when I was stirring the mac and cheese. "Hi, Mama," he said, sticking his finger in the pot for a taste. He smelled of Cynthia's perfume, and I scratched his scalp behind his ears the way he liked so he wouldn't see the worry on my face. The house was a mess. It would take me weeks to get it back to the way it was when I left and spent my days cleaning and cooking and growing my vegetables in the yard. Already I deeply missed being free of every single one of them.

Boom cocked his head to the side. "You okay?" he asked.

"I'm just glad to be home," I said. A lump grew in my throat, but I didn't dare ask about Cynthia. I was afraid to know.

Later the boys came through bringing in groceries and beer while I fried the chicken for the noon meal. The macaroni and cheese bubbled sweetly on the stove. I made enough for everybody and for leftovers besides. Nobody was paying attention to me so I slipped out to the garage where Cynthia's car was, the bumper crunched into a crooked smile. In the trunk I found the pharma samples covered in warning stickers. *Do not mix with alcohol! Do not exceed prescribed dosage!* I ground the pills into dust with a pestle I kept in the kitchen for making salsa. My hips were still warm from my reunion with Victor the night before. My eyes burned with tears I couldn't let fall. I hated what I was about to do, but I couldn't stay. I already tried leaving without hurting anyone, and it didn't take, so what choice did I have? I crushed enough to kill every one of them ten times over and was about to spoon the dust into the cheese sauce when Victor came up on me quietly. He pressed his thumb hard into my wrist. The pestle dropped, clanging against the pot. He dragged me to the family room where there was a crate for a dog we didn't have anymore, a German Shepard who died before I left. "Turn, Casey," he said, his face as unforgiving as the canyon's granite walls. "You better turn now or I'm putting you in there as a woman."

So I turned. My skin burned as fur popped through my skin. The soft tissues of my body twisted in brief flashing pain followed by blistering relief as if every joint had been pulled out of socket and then thunked back in all at once. I let my weeping free as Maximo's t-shirt and jeans fell to the dirty floor.

Victor was crying too as he latched the cage door shut upon me.

✳

Within a couple of days I learned not to chew on the metal bars. They would not yield, and I was tired of the taste of my own bloody gums. Victor leashed me for morning walks at first until the end of the week when the boys fell to dissolution and started drinking all day. They weren't eating right either with nobody to cook regular meals. They were making me witness that they were falling apart without me. I tried to keep my bathroom in one corner of the cage, afraid to draw attention to myself by whining, afraid Victor would decide to end me. Some days they forgot to feed me. At the end of the first week, my water bowl went dry, and I thought that was how I would die until Victor stumbled down the stairs in the middle of the night to fill it. Later with my stomach distended from drinking too much at once, I thought it was time to accept the fact that Cynthia was probably dead, and the tragedy of that made me lick at the metal wire bars for punishment.

The next night Victor crumpled to his knees beside the cage, whiskey coming off him like gas fumes. He pointed a gun at my forehead, his eyes empty of love. After a minute he wiped his nose with the back of his hand and went away. He wasn't going to shoot me that night, but some night he would, and as miserable as I was, I did not want to die.

*

The boys ran out of booze money in the middle of my second week in captivity so they went on a run to make some. They were gone a while when the truck rolled up the driveway. I lifted my head, wondering if Victor came back to kill me when no one was around. But it was Boom, and he wasn't alone. He held the front door open for a woman whose laugh I knew. Boom followed after her like a puppy as she crouched beside me. Cynthia.

"What a beautiful dog," she said. She put her face close to mine and winked. Then she was up and laughing in short yelps while he growled in his throat and led her upstairs. After they were done, she came down alone, languid and smiling. I couldn't see the kitchen, but there were chopping sounds and onions sizzling in butter. By the time the boys returned she had made enough spaghetti and meatballs for everyone to leave the table with a full belly.

Cynthia ignored me as she moved around a house that once was mine. There was something different about her. She was a lot less eager to impress than before. She just served the food, barely talking. I kept my head on my paws as the boys popped open their after-dinner beers. Cynthia cleaned the mess while they cranked their music loud and turned into dogs and ran in and out of the front door to piss outside.

Eventually she came into the living room absently brushing a streak of white dust from her apron and sat on the couch. The boys crowded around her like they used to do with me, and just like I used to, she stroked their furred backs and rubbed them under their chins. Victor rested his head on her thigh, and, inside my head, I begged her not to fall in love with him. Boom at least was sweet. Victor would use her until there was nothing left.

Cynthia scratched Victor between his ears. She continued to ignore me until he turned into a man and flopped to the floor unconscious. The speakers blared discordant rock guitars as each of the sleeping Dogs turned into men strewn across the sectional, the recliners, and the cushions on the floor. The main room turned into a tableau of naked men: some hairy, some bald, some shaved, some with paunches, others with the bunched-up muscles of bodybuilders, stinking of alcohol, end-of-the-day mentholated deodorant, bacon grease and cigarettes.

Cynthia stepped over the men and unlatched my cage. I leaned into her hand, my heart bursting as she caressed my face. She patted her thigh and though my legs were stiff from two weeks in the cage, I went to her side. I watched Victor, but his jaw was slack. He and the boys were still and cold, the room silent. Cynthia gave them more painkillers than they needed just to fall asleep. She gave them enough to stop their hearts. A growl rumbled in my chest. My own heart was changing from inside me as it broke in grief while also exalting to be free. It twisted and burned as Cynthia's body crackled before me, fur covering her skin like brushed velvet, her clothes falling away from her limbs. With her wet nose she nudged me to the open door and we ran into the dark woods, raising our voices to the moon together.

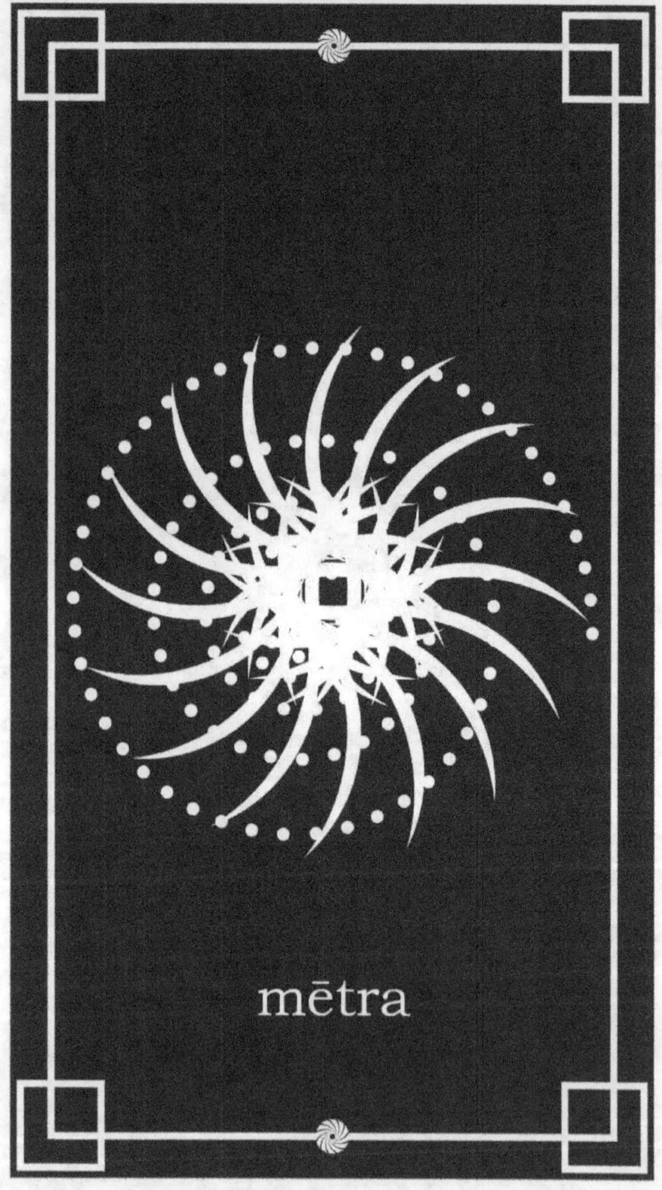
mētra

The Town Bike

LCW Allingham

The full Flower moon lit up the night, coating the midnight streets with light. The prom queen, the track star, the goth and the nerd walked together into Wakeman's Woods.

No one saw them. No one heard.

They followed ancient deer trails, brambles and stickers catching their ankles, bugs biting their thighs, but they didn't stop until they reached the creek where Samantha Soddenhook died.

"So, what do we do?" Liv, the goth, asked, staring at the flat rock where, twenty years ago, Samantha's naked body had been found. Arms and legs splayed, and her blood still wet on the ground.

They all knew the story; all heard it alike. Don't be like Samantha, don't be a town bike. Don't talk to strangers, be nice to boys, just keep your legs closed, don't play so coy, follow the rules, don't raise your voice, and don't go out at midnight, especially not with any boys.

"Um, I got the pigs blood," said the nerd, Bianca. She pulled out a pack of candles and a full bottle.

"The hair of her enemy." Catherine Lane kicked at the mud. Her voice was flat and hard as she pulled a baggie out of her pocket. She handed it to her best friend, Eva, state champ, who adjusted her knee brace while she laid it all out on the rock.

"It will work," Eva assured Cat and Cat buried her face.

Blood and flame and mud and hair. The girls spoke the words, to rock and wood, to water and wind, and the flame took it there.

Samantha Soddenhook, hear our call, we need our enemies to fall. We know you know the name we speak. We offer vengeance that you seek.

And the wind seemed to whisper the softest reply.

Hey Sammy, I want to take a ride.

The very last thing she heard before she died.

When the fire was done and the night was silent, the girls pushed the offerings, one by one, into the murky water.

"Do you think it worked?"

"We'll know soon enough."

"We'll catch up at lunch tomorrow." Catherine picked up her stuff.

They followed, one after another, down moonlit deer paths through Wakeman's woods.

Catherine took all their hands, and held them good and tight. These bonds had been forged in iron a month ago, on prom night.

Liv squeezed her hand back. "It's going to be fine."

"As long as you don't go out at midnight," Bianca joked from the back of the line.

In the still hours of the morning, they parted ways, prom queen, the track star, the goth and the nerd.

No one saw and no one heard.

That's always the case when girls go out at midnight. Their parents teach them what is right, their teachers tell them what is wrong. Their pastors, priests and mayor teach them that it's best to blend in, to hide.

Hey Sammy, I want to take a ride.

✳

At school, the AC didn't work, and the day was too hot. Boys took off their sweat soaked shirts. Girls who forgot the rules were sent to the office for letting their shoulders show. That's the way it goes.

Bianca, Liv, Eva and Catherine sat in the shade, ignoring the fuss their grouping made.

What's Cat and Eva doing with those weirdos? What's Bianca doing with those assholes? What's Liv doing there when she usually sits alone?

Some remembered days when the four were best friends, before they were ranked and pulled apart, pretty, gifted, weird, smart. Everyone filed and given a name.

But labels don't account for shared secrets of shame.

A prom night problem, only they saw. Then floodgates burst open and these girls told all of their troubles to each other again. Just like before Cat's mom got married and secrets divided them, way back when.

"Did you see your step dad this morning?" Eva asked.

Before Catherine could answer, Bianca yelped a warning.

A tall, well-built boy sauntered near, leaned down with a sneer. "Where were you last night, Cat? You were missed."

"Fuck off," Liv hissed.

He leaned toward Catherine, a breach in her guard. "You doing some kind of community outreach?"

Catherine shook. Bianca took her hand. Eva demanded, "I mean it, Davis, get the hell out of here! She doesn't want to talk to you!"

"Ooh, I'm getting reprimanded." The boy snorted. "Cat can speak for herself. Who are you? Her bodyguard?"

But Cat couldn't make her mouth work as she glared around the school yard. Couldn't make her hands move. Couldn't make her voice come up her throat. Couldn't stop the frozen fear that held her down to gloat.

"It was just a misunderstanding." His voice was in her ear. Like his intentions were all that mattered.

He reached his hand in. As soon as his thick fingers circled her wrist, Catherine's paralysis shattered.

She screamed and thrashed and hissed.

Her friends watched as Davis's eyes went wide, hearing the call from the other side.

First the cold, the frigid bite of newly thawed ice, pounding into his ears, eyes, nose, mouth. Then the rocks, scraping across his shoulder blades, grinding along his spine and side and finally, crack, right across the temple. Once, then twice.

Hey Sammy, I want to take a ride.

He dropped Catherine's wrist, but it was too late. He saw the eyes in the darkness. He heard the scrape of her nails across the stone. He staggered away. Nobody noticed the shadows at play. His buddies joked and jostled him until the bell and then he followed them to class where he fell to his knees, sweat dripping down his ruddy face.

Then blood from his nose, and he was staring into space. The ambulance came.

"Unresponsive," they said as they rolled him down the hall. "He's completely catatonic."

Davis wasn't there at all. He was somewhere else. With someone else.

"It's working," Eva muttered to Liv when they met up between bells.

✳

Mrs. Curie had noticed Bianca's conclusions always matched with Wes. But while his work was clean, her papers were full of false starts, crossed out work and mess. When Bianca accused Wes of cheating, Mrs. Curie paid it no mind, but in the last month his work had started to decline. She checked everything carefully to make sure that Wes's slot as valedictorian wasn't in peril.

And there in Bianca's work, those same wrong answers, cold, stark and sterile. She'd never looked so close before. It's the end of the year and Bianca was always smart enough but easy to ignore. She wasn't Ivy league material, not a star. Mrs. Curie knew *her* Wes would go far.

But his new work baffled her, tidy lines of equations that were total nonsense, as if he'd been using Bianca's mess as more than reference.

As if he'd been copying Bianca's work all year.

She called them both in, to get it all clear before graduation.

"Bee just helped me out." Wes smiled like a shark.

Bianca just stared, her eyes cynical and dark. They reminded the teacher of a girl in her own class, stupid piece of ass that made the boys act like idiots. Slut. Whore.

"You're going to help Wes correct his score," Mrs. Curie told Bianca. "Don't be petty about it."

Bianca shook her head and got herself ready. Then it took hold.

The cold, the frigid bite of newly thawed ice, pounding into their ears, eyes, nose, mouth. Then the rocks, scraping across their shoulder blades, grinding along their spines and sides and finally, crack, right across the temple. Once, then twice.

Hey Sammy, I want to take a ride.

They saw the eyes in the darkness, heard the scrape of her nails across the stone. Bianca left with the bell to go home. Mrs. Curie and Wes glared into the night, lost to the world, lost to the light.

✳

"Where's my star? Where's the girl they're all talking about?" Coach Norris came into the girl's locker room and the other runners cleared out. He reached for Eva's swollen knee and squeezed and the air within his lungs seemed to freeze. He felt the hot hands scrape up his side.

Hey Sammy, I want to take a ride.

✳

"When I call you, you pick up the phone. This isn't rocket science, you pig!" Ryan wasn't tall but he felt big as he loomed over Liv. "You need to obey and stop being combative!"

"I want to break up," Liv murmured, so soft she could barely hear herself.

His grip just got firmer until tears pooled in her eyes. He shouted, "And now here we go with the lies. What the hell, Liv? You're pathetic you know? Where do you think you could go?"

She jerked away and screamed, "I said STOP!"

He tasted blood on his lips and felt his ears pop. The hits bouncing back for each time that Liv cried.

Hey Sammy, I want to take a ride.

✳

Principal Puther sat across from the girls, a sympathetic smile on his skinny face. "I know you've all had a hard year, and I want to assure you this is a safe space."

Catherine snorted and Eva stared. Bianca rolled her eyes and Liv sat there, glaring at her hands. They'd all been in this office before with this man.

He understood their pain! He wished them all well! He felt super bad about the tales that they tell about Samantha Soddenhook, but you know what it's like—Nobody wants to be the town bike. He'd really tried to help her out, told her she'd get in trouble if she kept running about after midnight. Walking alone with boys.

Just keep your head down. Just don't raise your voice. Be a nice girl and you'll have a choice. Don't open your legs and don't make too much noise.

"Girls, what is happening?" the principal cried. "Three students, two teachers. They all almost died. They're all the ones you brought to my attention, and now they're all in the hospital!"

"Are you going to give us detention?" Liv had a bad attitude.

"I've been trying to help you!"

"I'm sorry, what?" Eva's tone was also rude. "By asking us to keep our mouths shut?"

"Until we could conduct an investigation." Principal Puther tried to exert his authority.

It's just that so many other things took priority.

"We didn't do anything and even if we did, how are you going to accuse the mayor's kid?" Eva asked.

Catherine stood up. "It's true. You know my step father never had to clean up a mess."

The other girls stood up to leave. Bianca shook her head. "Your *help* is worthless."

✳

Denise Lane regarded the girls with a worried knit of her brow. Catherine had been acting out, and now she'd invited these new girls here, weird girls, uncool girls. Girls that were bad. The kind of girls Denise had hung around with once. The kind of girls that made Andrew mad.

Something was wrong. The air felt thick and strange, like tension that would coil up just before a fight.

"You're not going anywhere tonight, right Cat?"

"No, Mom." Catherine lounged on the couch and didn't bother to look.

"Nice girls don't go around at midnight. You remember Samantha Soddenhook."

"Jesus Mom, you never stop."

Denise felt something inside her tremble and pop. Samantha Soddenhook. Sam. Sammy.

Best friends forever.

"It's been a rough week at school." Denise tried a new endeavor, as she leaned against the door. "All those people getting sick."

"They were already sick," Eva said. "Now they can't hurt anyone anymore."

Denise ignored her. "Have you checked in on Davis, Cat?"

"Davis can burn in hell," Catherine spat.

"Did you *know* Samantha, Mrs. Lane?" Bianca pulled a book down from the shelf..

Denise felt a little sick herself. "Girls like that...well you've heard the term the town bicycle."

"No." Liv's black rimmed eyes watched her from the side.

"Well, um, you know. A girl who's the town bicycle...everyone gets a ride."

"What time is Andrew coming home?" Catherine asked.

"Late. I don't know." Denise fiddled with her wedding ring.

"He was a grade above her." Eva stated like it proved something.

"We all went to school with her," Mrs. Lane said. "It was a shock."

Catherine sighed and looked at the clock. "You all talk about it like it was inevitable. Telling us to stay at home, or end up like her. It's just what happens to girls who go out at midnight, like they're looking for trouble. Samantha Soddenhook took a walk after dark with a boy or on her own. No one knows. No one saw. And when she screamed no one heard at all."

"When they found her body in the woods, people said they did her good. Police said it was open and shut. Beat, raped and drowned for being a slut," Eva said.

Mrs. Lane began to shake, her whole body over.

"And as for who did it, nobody cared. It was better to just keep the girls inside, scared. And keep them all quiet with stories like Samantha Soddenhook, the town bike," Bianca said.

"You girls don't stay up too late." Mrs. Lane scurried up the stairs, away from Cat and her terrifying friends. And the memories of her own friend, and her terrible fate.

✳

"It's working," Bianca said. "What do we do now?"

"We let it run its course," Cat confirmed. "It's how we agreed it would be. Are you all okay?"

They didn't have to say it. They recalled Cat's bloody dress, Eva's win on a torn meniscus, and Bianca's second best. They recalled bruises on Liv's arms and legs, and the people who were supposed to protect them, but instead sent them away with platitudes and lectures about how girls behave today.

"Do you think our parents will be okay?" Eva's voice was small.

No one knew the answer. They were not sure at all.

It turned out midnight was too late, Samantha walked at ten. She climbed up out of rock and mud, shook off bugs and brambles then moved through the town.

The friends who'd said it was what she'd deserved, the boys who'd groped at her curves, the teachers, pastors, priests and cops who'd said it was just what bad girls got, and that is what happens when you are a whore. They all found Samantha at their doors.

The boys who beat and the girls who shame, the ones who always spit her name, they all stared down the old deer path, and sunk into an icy bath.

And in their ears, they'd hear him sigh.

Hey Sammy, I want to take a ride.

✳

They had been friends in the early days. Played together before Catherine's mom had married Mr. Lane and moved her to his mansion and they'd all been pushed their separate ways.

Before that final parting, they'd been playing all alone, hide and seek through out the rooms of Andrew Lane's big home.

Liv found bloody underwear in Mr. Lane's desk drawer, along with the picture of Samantha Soddenhook. She called her friends to look. A secret they shared, because little girls don't know who to trust when they're scared.

They can't trust themselves. Not even with facts. The world tells them they act too emotional, they think whatever their silly minds like. That there's no way their beloved mayor murdered the town bike.

Be good docile girls. Don't talk about the dark. Don't walk after the dark. And if they leave a mark, don't speak their names. Good girls follow rules, and stay in their lanes.

Good girls get hurt by bad men anyway.

So, trauma and secrets can pull girls astray, but sharing it puts them together again.

And Samantha has just been waiting for when.

There was a rattle at the door and Andrew Lane burst in. The girls went up stairs to see where he'd been.

"Cat, get your mom. The whole town's gone to hell."

The wolf sharp edge to his teeth, the glint in his eye as his gaze grazed the girls in their pajamas. "Your friends can come as well."

Andrew Lane was a handsome man, a charming man, a man who'd never had to raise a hand to get what he wanted, and never had to suffer the consequences of mistakes.

There were lawsuits, buried, payoffs, interns and secretaries and even friends' wives who claimed Cat's stepfather had crossed the lines. But looks, charm and money made it so easy to fake.

Mayor Lane never had cause to miss a beat, but tonight something stalked the streets with her mouth on his name.

A knock came at the door, just behind Andrew Lane.

He jumped and looked at the girls. "Expecting someone?"

"Just one more friend," Catherine said. "She went on a snack run."

The other girls said nothing more.

Andrew was relieved. "I was worried some creep followed me home."

He opened the door.

Samantha Soddenhook smiled on the stoop, her broken teeth black and jagged. The left side of her face drooping. "Hey Andy, let's take a ride."

Andrew Lane stared, petrified. A gurgling rumbling from his throat where his voice was caught in terror. The girls all took hands and stepped back, bearers of Samantha's revenge.

"Just a quick walk, just a little fun. Maybe in the woods. It'll be a quick one. You know you're my boy, right? My baby boy. My sexy boy. It's always been you, no matter what they said." A piece of skull slid from the crushed part of her head.

"S—S—Sammy—"

Samantha Soddenhook reached out and curled her boney fingers around his neck, bringing his face down to hers. "We always have fun, don't we? You want it. Don't wreck it."

"Andrew!" Mrs. Lane had run down to look, and was frozen at the sight of Samantha Soddenhook.

"Hey Denise." Samantha's one yellowed eye rolled up to Mrs. Lane. "This nasty boy get you in his game?"

Denise jerked back, but she didn't go to Andrew. She finally understood. "I am so sorry for what was done to you."

Samantha looked from her to Catherine and then nodded her decaying head.

"Sammy!" Andrew should have played dead. "I don't—I didn't mean—It wasn't me, there—"

She turned back to him and she showed her black teeth in a horrible grin. She raked her fingers into his thick, graying hair. She wrapped her arms around his trim waist. She leaned her face to his, whispered in his ear. No one else was close enough to hear.

Then she dragged him through the door.

No one moved.

No one spoke.

No one stopped the horror.

Hey Andy, I want to take a ride.

The very last thing he heard before he died.

In the still hours of the morning, they walked a new town, a new street, a new future where they wouldn't be kicked down, the prom queen, the track star, the goth and the nerd.

No one saw and no one heard.

INCUBATE

akpannwa
INCUBATE

Motherhood Changes You

Dale W. Glaser

All hell was breaking loose inside Nicola McGowan. She was a raging beast, tearing the curtains off the bedroom windows, hurling the petite Tiffany lamp on her nightstand into the dead center of her vanity's mirror to unleash a burst of jagged shards, hoisting her hope chest overhead and sweeping it across the top of her husband Mark's dresser, sending everything on it including the television smashing to the hardwood floor. She visualized herself doing all of those things, at least, and further imagined the rampage finally rousing Mark from sleep, so she could scream at him, "Oh, did I wake you? Because Taylor's crying didn't do it for you. It woke me, and I haven't slept three consecutive hours in three days!"

Imagining it all, immersing herself in the fantasy's details, helped. A little. Enough to keep her on the right side of sane. This was new to her, hyper-vivid fantasizing about violent destruction. She couldn't recall having remotely similar thoughts before Taylor had been born, and now not only did they occur frequently, but they felt intuitive, an organic part of her. She might have spared some energy for introspection about it, but she had a squalling baby to deal with, which was where her focus needed to be.

Nicola rolled out of bed, quietly and gently, leaving Mark sprawled and snoring on the mattress's opposite side. Justified in her fury or not, the rational part of her mind knew she was better off keeping it to herself. They had struck a bargain, after all, and he was holding up his end. She needed to do the same, and if she found that difficult at times, exhausting, even excruciating, she needed to suffer in silence. Not part of the bargain, exactly, but it certainly seemed to be the spirit Mark had intended.

She padded the few steps down the hall to the nursery door. Taylor was not just crying, he was full-on freaking out, legs thrashing inside his fleece sleep sack, tiny fists balled and shaking, eyes screwed shut and mouth wide open, every breath a rapid rattling lament, like someone revving an emotionally devastated chainsaw: uhuh-AHHAH-uhuh-AHHAH. A paranoid current slithered down her spine, insisting that something terrible had happened, that someone had done this to her baby, someone had been in the nursery and might be there even now, trying to mask their nefarious presence.

Nicola resisted the urge to peer into the dark corners of the room, chiding herself for being ridiculous. She bent over the crib rail and lifted Taylor to her shoulder. Some days she felt like she hadn't learned anything in five months of being a new mother. Nothing had gotten easier, and a few things had managed to get harder. One lesson had stuck: when Taylor was this worked up, he needed a minute of soothing before even beginning to address the root cause. She rubbed his back, swiveled her upper body back and forth and countered his panicky sobbing with slow, steady shushes. Gradually his wailing subsided to whimpering, and only then did Nicola shuffle her way to the gliding rocker in the corner. She sat down, arranged the nursing pillow on her lap and laid Taylor across it. She took off her nightshirt and guided her baby's mouth to her nipple.

Taylor fed, half-heartedly, as if it were a comforting distraction and not the reason he had woken up. While he nursed, Nicola unzipped his sleep sack and felt the front of his diaper, which was flat, thin and cool. She gave him a few minutes to nurse, then returned him to her shoulder and burped him. A tiny bubble of gas escaped his lips, not nearly enough to have woken him up.

Nicola returned Taylor to his crib and stood for a moment looking down at him. He appeared peaceful, but she knew it was fragile and fleeting. He might wake up again in an hour, or two hours, or twenty minutes. She wished she knew what he wanted, what he needed. He ruined her sleep like it was his job, but that wasn't a helpful way of thinking. It felt that way, but that was the sleep deprivation talking. Babies didn't torture their parents for the sake of torture. They were helpless little proto-humans with extremely limited resources.

Nicola was the adult, she told herself as she crawled back into bed beside Mark. It was her job to figure things out, to give Taylor what he needed. She could ask for help too, she realized. Not from Taylor, and not from Mark, a bargain was a bargain, but maybe elsewhere. She held onto that solace as she fell asleep.

※

The next day, while Mark was at work, Nicola drove Taylor across town to Shelly Wilton's house for their weekly get-together. The gathering went by different names according to the various attendees. Shelly called it a group playdate, even though Taylor was still too young to really play with the other children, and the kids who were old enough to play together ignored each other as often as not. Megan DeGarmo called it mommy club, closer to the truth in Nicola's opinion, an opportunity for the mothers to socialize and indulge in too-rare adult conversation. Vera Jesenska called it SAHM time, which Nicola only knew began with four capital letters because she had once asked Vera to explain the joke, and Vera had told her that internet forums on parenting used acronyms galore, like SAHM for stay-at-home mom.

Not every mom made it to Shelly's every week, but this time the quartet was complete. Nicola sat on the edge of the sofa in Shelly's large living room, Taylor seated on the floor in front of her, clutching one of Nicola's index fingers in each chubby fist and alternately staring around the room and trying to jam her fingers in his mouth.

"So, it's totally normal to go a few days without sleep when they're this age, right?" Nicola asked the room, choosing her words with deliberation. "Totally normal, right?" was a code among the mothers to indicate they wanted reassurance and not judgment, from Megan's "It's totally normal to never want to have sex with your husband unless you get a little drunk, right?" to Shelly's "It's totally normal to wish death on your mother-in-law when the only help she offers is brutal criticism, right?"

"Do you mean night sleep, or naps?" Shelly asked from her overstuffed chair, bottle-feeding her daughter Kayleigh and watching her two-and-a-half-year-old son Spencer play on the floor with various rescue vehicles that had large-eyed, grinning faces. Kayleigh was five months old, two days younger than Taylor; Nicola and Shelly had met sharing a recovery room after giving birth in the same hospital. "They sleep when they're tired, one way or the other."

Nicola was about to ask who they were, then bit her lip in embarrassed realization. "I meant me," she admitted.

Shelly tilted her head to the side. "Can't Mark take over for one night and let you sleep?"

"Ha," Vera scoffed dryly. She sat cross-legged on the floor, her nine-month-old Dania napping between her knees and her four-year-old Xander sitting beside her, flipping through a book. "Men can help make babies, and pay for college. Everything in between is on us."

Nicola smiled at that, mostly because it spared her from having to explain the bargain. "It seems like it's midnight feedings Taylor wants."

"So pump some during the day and let Mark give him a bottle overnight," Shelly suggested. "Or do formula, I know, I know, but just once, so you can get a good night's sleep."

Nicola shook her head. "It's not food in his belly, it's...the act of nursing? I don't know, you'll say I'm crazy, but it's like he wants something from me, and I can't figure out what it is. And I feel like I'm supposed to be able to, like I should already know it, and there must be something wrong with me, it's like he wants something from my body other than milk but it's not my body, or I'm not connected to it anymore..." She hastily swiped away a tear escaping her left eye.

"Oh, sweetie, hang in there," Megan said from the opposite end of the couch, her hands wrapped loosely around a mug of oolong tea. Her fourteen-month-old, Emma, made wobbly circuits walking from Megan to her diaper bag across the room and back again. Each time Emma carried a new toy, which she would hand to Megan and trade for the previous one to carry back to the diaper bag. "Taylor's almost six months, right? He'll be sleeping through the night on his own soon, and so will you, you're so close."

"Did any of you ever feel that way?" Nicola asked. "Like you didn't recognize your own body anymore?"

"You mean the body with stretch marks on its stomach, and hair falling out in the shower?" Vera asked.

Nicola laughed and sniffled at the same time. "Point taken."

"I think everybody has something, though," Shelly said. "Smells never used to bother me physically, if I didn't like the way something smelled, I just didn't stay around it too long, but then once I had Spencer, anything too strong made me weak in the knees, sick to my stomach. Including some things I used to love! Completely lost my taste for scallops, and I remember turning them down once and thinking, *Who am I?*"

"Mmm-hmmm, I had almost the opposite thing happen," Megan added. "I used to not care much for chocolate, Keith was the chocolate lover, but now I crave it every few weeks. It's like he passed the sweet tooth down to Emma, and while I was carrying her in my body, she passed it over to me. Crazy."

Nicola considered Shelly and Megan's points, remembering a night not long before...a week ago? Two weeks? Time had blurred. She had made a pork tenderloin for dinner and Mark had complained that it had been nearly raw in the center. The whole thing had turned into a big fight, with Mark accusing her of being so negligent they were both likely to get food poisoning. She had tried to apologize, but he had doubled down, because he had been keeping an eye on Taylor at the time so Nicola could cook dinner. And if she couldn't pay close enough attention to get the meat cooked all the way through, what was the point? In the aftermath of hurt feelings and petty sniping as the fight slowly burned out, Nicola felt a strange kind of shame because the few bites of tenderloin she'd taken had been delicious, maybe the best she'd ever tasted. She attributed the obliviousness to brain-numbing fatigue, but was it possible after pregnancy and delivery she had developed a tolerance, even an unhealthy preference, for raw pork?

"Mergency! Mergency!" Spencer yelled, derailing Nicola's train of thought. He was crawling fast on his hands and knees, pushing his cartoony ambulance in a wild serpentine path which ultimately crossed a page of Xander's book and tore it out. Xander howled in protest and jerked the book away, startling Spencer, who burst into tears. Vera tried to settle Xander down without waking Dania, while Shelly got up and laid Kayleigh in a baby seat, setting off crying from the baby. Belatedly, Megan set her tea down and rose to help.

Nicola watched it all unfold and felt nothing beyond annoyance and disgust at the children's weakness. They didn't deserve to be coddled over their tears; they barely deserved to live.

The thought shocked her like a wave of cold water, and she rejected it immediately, terrified the other moms would somehow sense it had passed through her mind. She wondered if this playdate should be her last.

*

Mark called after work and announced he'd be picking up dinner on his way home, struck by a sudden craving for Pad Thai. It was one of his ways of buttressing his side of the eternal argument over pulling his weight and doing his fair share of the parenting. Yes, Nicola cooked every night, but once or twice a month Mark would spare her the trouble by bringing home takeout, and that evened things out. He'd never used the word 'craving' in any context before Taylor was born either, another example of his all-in-this-together solidarity with Nicola, as far as Mark was concerned. A two-for-one, from Mark, the modern master of efficiency.

Never mind that after dinner, Mark still expected Nicola to clear the table, load the silverware into the dishwasher and find room for leftovers in the refrigerator. By then he'd done his part, and couldn't be expected to help with the cleanup. Instead he got down on the floor for his daily ten minutes of interaction with Taylor.

Nicola silently accepted all of this, as always. Once the table was wiped down, the dishwasher started, and leftovers packed away, Nicola leaned against the wall to observe Daddy-Taylor playtime. Taylor was on his back on a pastel-rainbow playmat, and Mark dangled a floppy stuffed dog above him, making barking noises. Whenever Taylor looked away, Mark would change to growling noises and jiggle the toy under Taylor's chin until Taylor laughed.

Nicola felt a sudden stirring of desire. She wanted the thrill of someone growling in her ear while ravishing her. Not by Mark, who had shown even less sexual interest in her since Taylor's birth, despite rarely demonstrating any before. This was the opposite of wanting Mark, a lusting for anyone else but Mark, to feel desirable and experience pleasure and also punish Mark all in one fell swoop of infidelity. She felt her face flush and hurried to the sink for a glass of cold water. With deep shame, she told herself it was a momentary lapse into a completely alien impulse. She almost convinced herself, except for an impossible yet insistent sensation that the impulse was as much memory as fantasy.

✳

Nicola had let go of most of her guilt over her uncharitable views of her friends' kids and her husband by the middle of the night, as she nursed Taylor at 1:16 a.m. Taylor clawed at the top of her breast, his tiny fingernails annoyingly sharp, until Nicola laid her finger in his palm. He squeezed powerfully.

The scratches reminded Nicola of her shower earlier in the evening. Bathing herself was a rare treat, between meeting Taylor's bottomless needs, keeping the house from falling into utter disarray, and occasionally managing to sleep and feed herself. Nicola honestly didn't mind skipping a day or two of bathing, but her leg hairs had been itching like mad recently. She'd started the water and grabbed a pink disposable razor, then stepped around the curtain, barely giving the first droplets a chance to cascade all the way down her backside before lathering up her legs. She'd worked speedily and suffered a couple of nicks. The potential for bloodletting was one of the things she'd always hated about shaving her legs, hence she'd been thrilled to receive laser hair removal as a birthday present from Mark shortly before Taylor's conception. Nicola also gave her armpits a few quick swipes and cut her left side pretty badly. The bleeding had stopped quickly, but there was a lot of red for a few moments, and Nicola thought she might have torn off a skin tag.

Now, sitting in the dark in the nursery with a moment to collect her thoughts, she belatedly pondered how her leg and armpit hairs were growing back after permanent laser removal. Why hadn't it occurred to her before how odd that was? The obvious answer was that very little beyond basic day-to-day survival registered with her lately. The effort required to sneak in a hurried shower drained her, and nothing else could penetrate her sleep-deprived brain fog. Mental math utterly escaped her. Could she even be sure it was earlier that evening she had cut herself in the shower? Was she remembering some other long-ago shaving mishaps?

She moved her right hand to her left armpit, slowly, so as not to jostle Taylor as he suckled. Her fingertip found the fresh scab there, rough yet fragile, and worried at it until it peeled away. Nicola withdrew her finger and saw, in the pale streetlamp illumination, the glint of fresh blood.

Taylor unlatched and mewled at her. Impulsively Nicola stuck her finger in the baby's mouth, and he sucked on it greedily, tiny tongue rasping at the pad. She pulled her finger away, saw the blood was gone, and swore she heard Taylor sigh contentedly. She looked at him and, for a moment, couldn't register what she was seeing. Taylor was sound asleep, eyes closed, lips parted, breathing deep and regular. Nicola couldn't remember Taylor ever dropping so deeply so quickly. But it was hard to remember yesterday, impossible to dredge up the day before that.

Nicola transferred Taylor back to his crib, and he continued his untroubled sleep. As she padded quietly back to her and Mark's bed, she told herself she was due for one easy midnight feeding. Every other mom had stories about their babies wearing themselves out and falling asleep at the drop of a hat, just like every other mom had stories about food aversions and allergies. Maybe Taylor had finally turned a corner, and maybe things were going to get easier. Maybe she would miss the midnight feedings when they were gone.

Even if he hadn't reached some developmental milestone, even if tonight had been a fluke, whatever had just happened had nothing to do with her baby tasting her blood. She willed herself to fall asleep, ignoring the hot twinges in the back of her mouth at the corner of her jaw.

※

Nicola called her mother the next day. They spoke on the phone about once a week, a situation that Nicola took for granted. Nicola asked after her father and her mother asked after Mark, and then the conversation turned to Taylor, as had become the new normal. Once she had delivered the requisite updates from Taylor sitting up all by himself to his midnight nursing demands, Nicola said, "Mom, can I ask you something?"

"Of course," her mother said.

"After I was born, when I was about Taylor's age, did you feel like you had changed?"

Her mother laughed. "That would be an understatement. Once you have a child, everything is different. Everything revolves around them, and keeping them safe and happy, or at least content enough to give you a moment's peace now and then."

"Right, but like, was that you changing, physically?"

"I suppose you could say I saw the world through different eyes," her mother mused. "I thought about things from your point of view and not just my own."

"Right, right, but Mom, I mean like did you notice anything about your own body, that you didn't expect, that didn't seem like it had anything to do with the pregnancy except it wasn't there before you had me but it was there after?"

"That...doesn't exactly ring a bell," her mother said. "Can you give me an example? What's going on with you?"

"Nothing, it's just...I don't know," Nicola said, deflating.

"Is it good or bad?" her mother pressed. "I do remember when you were a little older than Taylor, around your first birthday, it occurred to me that I had become much more productive. Nothing that would revolutionize the world, but when your father and I were first married, he would go to work, I would stay home, and I would clean the house and run some errands and always have some time for myself in the afternoon just to rest and enjoy myself before I started making dinner. Then along came you and away went the lazy afternoons, but by the end of that first year I didn't even miss them. In fact, I was probably getting more done every day even though I had to juggle you into the mix. And I felt a little guilty about that, about how much I could have gotten done before if I hadn't been indulging in those quiet afternoons...I don't know if that makes much sense. Your father certainly didn't understand, he told me I was being silly."

"I'm sure Daddy just meant it was silly for you to feel guilty," Nicola said.

"Well, be that as it may," her mother said, "I certainly didn't expect to have more energy as a mother of a toddler than I did when I was a young newlywed, but that's what happened."

"Right."

"I don't want to pry, but I'm sorry if that's not what you wanted to hear," her mother said.

"No, it's fine, Mom," Nicola said, and added, unable to stop herself, "I'm just tired, is all. Tired and feeling weird."

"Make sure you sleep whenever Taylor sleeps," her mother said, which Nicola felt like she was hearing for the millionth time. "And try giving him a bowl of rice cereal mixed with warm milk for dinner, to get him to sleep longer."

"OK, Mom," Nicola said. "Love you, love to Daddy."

After they hung up, Nicola squeezed her right hand into a fist. Her nails dug into the flesh of her palm, sharp and hard. She could feel them, aware of the tension in her clenched finger muscles, the sensation of pain shooting back up the nerves to her brain. It was still her body, she was in control of its movements and actions, and she was at the center of all of its receptor signals. If it didn't always feel familiar, maybe that didn't matter. Things changed, people changed, bodies could change too, but she was still Nicola. New body or old it was hers.

She wanted to drive her fist through something, too. Nothing specific, anything that would make a satisfying crunch and be left ruined would do.

Taylor cried, as if to remind her that he needed her, he had a claim on her body as well. Even though she was beyond exhausted, weary down to her bones, and mystified as to where the urges to punch and wreck had come from, she rose to answer his cry.

*

Nicola sat in the glider while Taylor suckled at her breast. The darkened nursery was not just a room, it was a sphere untouched by time, a void in the passage of minutes into hours. While the world slept, and the sun hid its face, the nursery floated in static, perpetual quiet. The patchwork elephant quilt hanging on the wall, the tiny rocket ships and stars dancing on the ends of their strings that formed the mobile over Taylor's crib, the changing table in desperate need of organization, cluttered with wipes and ointments and burp cloths on top and overflowing bins of clothes and pajamas on the shelves, all were ageless witnesses to the ritual of mother and son. The night was a vast ocean of mystery all around, with no way of knowing if one shore of it or another were closer to where she rocked on its perpetual waves. It might be only minutes after eleven o'clock, only moments after she had fallen asleep beside Mark; it might be later than five o'clock, dawn rushing on without pity. It was impossible to determine, and meaningless. It was night.

Nor did it matter which night it was, the night following her last phone call with her mother, or the night after her razor had drawn blood in the shower. Perhaps those were both the same night, it was impossible to differentiate.

Nicola surrendered to the abiding feeling of time suspended, because it felt somehow familiar. She had felt like this before, and not too long ago. She retraced the passage of days and nights back through memory, all the way back to the time before motherhood, to the mentally and emotionally grueling effort of trying to conceive. Nicola had stared down many sleepless nights, lying in bed and wondering what was wrong with her, why this everyday biological occurrence which befell irresponsible teenage girls every day was proving impossible for her.

But at least those sleepless nights had served a purpose, forcing her to muster her courage and broach the subject of infertility with Mark. He hadn't wanted to talk about it, of course, he insisted dwelling on it was giving in to negativity when what they needed was to stay positive. It would happen when it happened, they had just had some bad luck so far. But Nicola, in a rare display of opposition, had pushed forward and asked what if it wasn't just luck, what if there was something else at fault, a scientific problem with a medical solution.

Mark had been adamantly opposed to any kind of fertility treatment, and they had maintained a tense impasse over it for months, until finally Nicola had said if they didn't take action soon it might be too late. Mark had shocked her by saying maybe if it couldn't happen without them taking action, it was a sign that it wasn't meant to be. For several days Nicola had confronted the potential breaking point of their marriage, Mark's dismissive callousness about her desire to become a mother. She had come very close to leaving him.

In the end Mark had relented. Somewhat. They had struck their bargain. Mark agreed to one attempt at fertility treatment, and whether it succeeded or failed it would fall on Nicola to deal with the consequences. If she had lost that pregnancy, there would be no second try. If it worked, but there were any complications, Nicola would bear the responsibility for them. Mark would give in, give her what she wanted, but in exchange she would fully accept whatever the outcome might be.

Taylor had been the outcome, healthy and precious and perfect and infuriating and intoxicating and utterly draining. Nicola had refused to surrender the idea that she would one day be a mother with a baby of her own and so had surrendered everything else, her freedom, her sense of time, her sense of self. If she didn't start sleeping better her health would start to suffer, she knew it.

She might lose her mind, and Mark, per their arrangement, would simply let it happen.

Taylor unlatched and fussed. Nicola gently turned him around on the nursing pillow and guided him to the opposite nipple. "It's not your fault, sweetie," she whispered in the eternal darkness. "Mommy will be all right. Mommy will find a way to be all right."

✳

"For what it's worth, I'm sorry," Nicola said into the phone. "I don't think I ever apologized at the time."

"For what?" Kylie asked, sounding genuinely confused.

"The end of our lease," Nicola said, adding lamely, "and…everything."

"Oh, honey, that's water under the bridge," Kylie said, unbothered. "I hope you haven't been avoiding me because of that. I just assumed, you know, newlywed life, you got busy, I got busy, and I heard through the grapevine you had a baby last year, congrats."

"Thanks," Nicola said. She wondered if Kylie really had let go of the past, or if she simply didn't want to devote any emotional energy to rehashing it. Nicola remembered the series of events with chagrin, how she had met Mark not long after she and Kylie had moved into a post-college apartment together, how the plan had been to split rent while Nicola worked full time as an HR administrator and Kylie went to medical school, but then things with Mark had moved so fast and in less than a year they were making plans to get married and move in together, leaving Kylie in the lurch. Nicola and Kylie had been close friends in college and then Kylie hadn't even come to Nicola's wedding, claiming it was a pure scheduling conflict though Nicola had always suspected more resentment. And so they had drifted apart, but Nicola had resolved to call her old friend out of a mounting sense of desperation. "I...it's been great but it's been hard, actually. Like, really hard."

"Oh, I'm sorry to hear that," Kylie said. "Postpartum depression is no joke. Have you talked to your doctor?"

"Not really," Nicola admitted, and laughed weakly. "But I'm talking to a doctor, right now."

"I'm...look, Nicola, are we being honest with each other here?"

"I'd like to think so," Nicola said, bracing herself for Kylie to finally unload on her over their falling out.

Instead, Kylie said, "It can be hard to talk about the personal stuff with your doctor, even the doctor who's seen you naked and pushing another human being out of your body. I get that, and I get how it could be easier to talk to me. And we can talk, fine, but you have to promise me you understand a chat on the phone is not the same thing as seeking actual medical counsel, right? We can break the ice but promise me you will also talk to your doctor, okay?"

"I promise," Nicola said.

"All right. Ask away," Kylie said.

"I don't feel depressed," Nicola said, dragging each word up and out of herself like lost objects at the bottom of a cold, black lake. "But I feel...off? Not myself. And I just don't know where the line is, you know? I'm tired...so, so tired...like, duh, everyone with a newborn is tired, but it makes it so hard to understand what else is happening to me. And I know on some level my life has changed, I didn't used to be a mom, now I am. Taylor wasn't a part of my life, now he's the central part, but like I said, where is the line between my life and me? There's these changes all around me and they affect me, but am I still me? Like, how would I even talk to my doctor about that? Is there some test they can run that says, you're seventy-eight percent someone else now? Some supplement to regrow the missing parts of me?"

"Right," Kylie said, and in her mind, Nicola could see her former roommate tapping the edge of her chin with her forefinger the way she always did in deep thought. "Look, on the one hand, I do not know what it's like to give birth, personally. But I know there's some truth in what you're saying, all of it. Pregnancy and delivery are some of the most extreme, physiologically demanding circumstances a human body can be put through, and every bored hippie with a blog is out there telling the world it's natural, it's easy, don't take drugs, don't go to a hospital, but it's not that easy, it's always going to have risks. Sorry, that's my personal soapbox, but my point is that gets in your head, right? All these little cottage industries and self-proclaimed experts saying it should be a breeze and doctors focusing on the other end of it, mitigating the worst-case scenarios, and those mixed messages probably leave you pretty unsettled, huh?"

"I guess so."

"We evolved to have babies this way, but we also adapted to it," Kylie went on. "Almost every mother will survive childbirth. You did. The mothers who thrive are the ones who then have help, from doctors, or partners or the baby's grandparents. It takes a village and all. Do you have that kind of support?"

"Well…yes," Nicola said. "I could probably ask for more, accept more."

"I know it's hard, but yeah, I feel like that's the best advice I could give you."

"Any second-best advice?"

"Embrace the change," Kylie answered. "Things are different now, and maybe you are too, just try to accept it. Not everything's going to be the way it used to be, but it's not supposed to be. For anybody, not just you, you've had a major change in your life recently, but everyone deals with little changes all the time. I mean, if every day you were exactly the same as the day before, and the day before that, and the day before that, on and on, you'd still be a baby like Taylor, right?"

"Some days I wish I was," Nicola said.

Kylie laughed. "Oh, don't we all. Listen I've got to run but it was good catching up with you. Call your doctor, take care of yourself, and don't be a stranger, all right?"

"All right," Nicola agreed. She set down her phone and thought for a moment about all the things she hadn't told Kylie. The unspoken words inside her sat somewhere between her heart and her stomach, mired in a cavity full of bile. Her legs itched, and her armpits itched, and her brain itched, but the thoughts were so heavy they were impossible to confess. That afflicted her the most.

Taylor cried angrily, and she went to him.

✳

Nicola's eyes jolted open. She stared at the ceiling above her and Mark's bed, and even though the room was filled with the darkness of the middle of the night, she could make out every bubble in the white paint, every strand of cobweb where the ceiling met the wall.

Something felt amiss, and for several moments Nicola felt a vertiginous confusion trying to put a finger on exactly what it was. She sat up and realized what was wrong: nothing.

Nothing was wrong at all. For the first time in far longer than she could remember, she didn't feel hungry, or dirty, or sore or itchy. She didn't even feel tired. She had only gone to bed a few hours ago but felt as though she had slept for an entire day and somehow regained all of her energy and then some. She half-expected herself to start crying in relief, but her emotions weren't as raw as they had been, either. She felt good, and felt grateful for feeling good.

Nicola swung her legs over the mattress's side and stood up. Mark snored, and the house's heating system sighed air through the vents, but otherwise all was quiet. She had woken up rejuvenated, and not because Taylor was crying for her. All the same, she felt the urge to tempt fate and check in on him.

She walked down the hall, her footsteps light and silent, feeling like walking on air. When was the last time she had felt this good? Not once since Taylor had been born, or any time during that dark stretch when she and Mark had been trying to conceive, except of course...the memory had been just at the edge of her mind's grasp, but then eluded her. It was a strange moment of deja vu, as if she had been trying to pin down the same memory for weeks or months but the brain fog of her fatigue and despair had not only made retrieving it impossible but had always immediately made her forget trying to recall. Now she felt sure it would come to her at any moment.

Nicola lingered on the nursery threshold, not wanting to disturb Taylor's sleep if she could help it. Every detail of the room stood out, even in the darkness, in crystal blue clarity. Through the slats of Taylor's crib, she could see the fuzzed curve of his head, the steady rise and fall of his chest. The baby wanted for nothing.

She had been so sure she sensed a need, though. If not Taylor's, then whose? Her own? Nicola barely stopped herself from laughing out loud at the mere thought of paying any attention to her own needs. She had been living entirely for Taylor, and before that, for Mark, winning him over to the bargain. She couldn't recall the last time she had given a fleeting consideration to herself, except of course...it was closer this time, brushing against her consciousness before floating away.

For a moment Nicola considered returning to bed, a thought met immediately by an almost dizzying wave of certainty that she should stay in Taylor's nursery. Something ineffable compelled her to remain, and her eyes drifted from the crib to the window full of moonlight.

That was what finally caught the memory and held it like a sharp steel hook, the ghostly luster of the moonlight, exactly as it had been that night some fifteen months ago.

She had spent most of the day at the fertility clinic. Despite all the snapshots of happy infants representing success stories on the walls, it was a cold, clinical, dehumanizing place, white walls and white coats, fluorescent lights and examination tables. As badly as Nicola wanted a baby, she had hated going to the clinic. She always went alone. As per their bargain, Mark refused to set foot inside after the one visit required for his sample collection.

When Nicola saw couples in the waiting room or the hallways, some happily optimistic, others hoping against hope, but all facing the future in solidarity, she hated the clinic that much more. Mostly because she hated Mark a little bit but couldn't bring herself to admit it. She'd tried to explain it to Mark that night, to articulate an inexorable sense of dread that the fertility treatment wasn't going to work in part because Mark wasn't involving himself. He had immediately deployed his usual defense: if it didn't work they should both take it as a given it wasn't meant to be. The fight had escalated until they were both screaming, then not speaking to each other, and Nicola had gone to bed early. She was still awake when Mark came to their room later, stretching out and falling asleep beside her almost immediately. She was still awake long after.

Eventually she had risen from bed and wandered to their spare room. It hadn't been a nursery then, just a haphazard combination of computer desk, daybed and random boxes making it a home office, guest room and storage space. The moonlight had fallen through the window just so. Nicola had held out her hand, allowing the moonbeam to lend its white glow to her flesh. She waited, as if she would be able to feel the silvery light pouring through her fingers and she could take something from it, or something could take her cares from her if she offered them up.

When she felt another hand take hold of her own, she had not been frightened. She had not even been surprised, as every moment unfolded as it had been meant to all along. First she felt the strong, reassuring grip, then she saw the hand holding hers. Her eyes traced from the wrist up the muscular arm to the broad chest and then to the handsome face, a knowing smile and dark mesmerizing eyes. He seemed impossibly tall, until Nicola looked down and realized he was floating a foot above the spare room's floor. She had no idea who he was, or how he had gotten into the house, or how he defied gravity, but she didn't care. In casting her sight downward she realized he was nude, and every inch of his physique was perfect, but her eyes were inexorably drawn back to his intense gaze. "Tell me what you desire most," he said.

She had wanted to say, "a baby" or "to be a mother." She had intended to, but the whispered words that passed through her lips, like the pre-ordained litany of an ancient ritual, were "to know the fullness of my womanhood," and those words were the ones he needed to hear, to pull her closer to him, to lift her up and draw her naked flesh against his.

She had no memory of taking off her night clothes, she was simply ready, she clung to him, and he held her up, and she opened to him, and there was pain but also pleasure. Pleasure like she had never known. She had bitten his shoulder to stifle the gasps of delight and moans of ecstasy, bitten so hard she was sure she would pierce his skin and taste the coppery tang of his blood at any moment. But he seemed impervious to harm, so she fastened her teeth to him and reveled in his smell, and his taste, and the kneading of his hands and every sensation inside her.

When they had both spent themselves, he laid her on the daybed, and she quivered as he separated from her. Nicola had felt as if her heart would race and her nerves would cry out for more forever, and yet not only had she fallen asleep moments later, she awakened in the morning in bed beside Mark, in her night clothes. It had all been nothing but a dream.

Nicola shook her head, bringing herself back to the present, once again seeing Taylor's nursery for what it was, not the chaotic room at cross-purposes with itself where she had once fantasized a wild erotic encounter, but a tidy den of tranquility, everything in its place. Except for Nicola's night clothes in a rumpled pile in the middle of the floor. Had she stripped in her reminiscence? She must have, and now she admitted to herself that however good she had been feeling when she woke, she felt even better now, completely unencumbered.

She braced her hands on her hips and arched her back, then bent forward to touch her toes, mildly amazed at the ache-free ease with which her body moved. She ran her hands up and down her legs, and found the hair had grown back again, all of it and more, long sharp quills standing out from her knees to her ankles. She stretched her arms up over her head and felt pops, one-two-three, along her ribs, then four-five from the undersides of her arms. She admired the fanlike wings spreading from her elbows to her waist, membranous skin stretched between pointed spines.

In the crib, Taylor had turned his head toward her. His eyes were open, regarding her with intelligent curiosity. There was no fear at what his mother had become, only a rumination on what she might do next.

Nicola crossed the room and lifted Taylor from the crib. His small body practically thrummed in her arms, straining with hunger and need, but not for mother's milk. She had misunderstood for so long, but now she knew what her baby had been trying to tell her. She laid him on the changing table, delicately unsnapped and unzipped his sleep sack with fingers tipped by curved black talons. She returned Taylor to her shoulder and felt a profound comfort at the searing heat of his flesh against hers.

She walked back to her bedroom, where Mark lay on his right side tangled in the bedsheets. Nicola rolled Mark onto his back and slid the sheets down to his waist, thankful her husband slept only in mesh gym shorts. She lowered Taylor to the crook of Mark's arm, face down.

Taylor raised his arms and scraped his tiny fingernails against the exposed skin of Mark's chest. Nicola had trimmed them after Taylor had scratched her, though she couldn't remember how long ago that had been, but they were razor sharp once again. Blood beaded from the thin lacerations and Taylor lapped at the ruby droplets, while Mark winced in his sleep. Taylor continued to dig at Mark's chest, wriggling insistently against Mark's ribcage as if intent on burrowing through the tissue, into the cavity within. Mark swatted absently at the baby with his opposite arm and shook his head back and forth against his pillow.

Nicola reached down and wrapped her fingers around Mark's throat. His eyes flew open, fully awake, but Nicola held him pinned in place. Mark's hands gripped Nicola's forearm, trying to pull her hand away, but she was stronger than him. She realized she had always been stronger than him.

Taylor clung tenaciously to Mark's side, turning the skin from Mark's collarbone to sternum to lowermost rib into a riot of bright red slashes. Mark, in wide-eyed choking panic, beat Nicola's elbow with his fists and twisted from side to side in an effort to shake Taylor off. Nicola tightened her grip, flexing muscles like steel cables, talons sinking deep into Mark's neck.

Mark stopped trying to punch Nicola's arm and instead clutched at his crushed windpipe. She drew her hand back and allowed the blood to flow freely from the puncture wounds. Mark stared at her in horrified disbelief for a moment before his eyes rolled back in his head. Blood ran down his neck and chest toward Taylor, who eagerly suckled at the scarlet streaks. Nicola licked blood from her talons as she watched Taylor with pride. Mark was shaking with paroxysms, but every drop of blood Taylor swallowed made him stronger. He would not be denied his ultimate prize. Nicola beamed at her son, her beautiful, perfect baby boy, as he pried apart Mark's exposed ribs with crimson stained hands and ferociously devoured Mark's heart. Gouts of blood washed over Taylor and soaked the bed as Mark finally fell still, and Nicola sighed, knowing only sublime happiness in what she had brought forth into the world, and what she had become.

rahim

INCUBATE

A Hole Where Your Back Should Be

Sofia Tantono

With variations, some of the events and one piece of dialogue presented here are inspired by a real-life occurrence and the discourse it inspired on social media.

It was by sheer willpower that she killed herself in childbirth.

In truth, the chances of Ayu giving birth to a healthy baby and living a normal life for an unmarried mother—one full of shame, ridicule, judgement, poverty and pity—were pretty good. But she had other plans, and it was these plans that kept her going as she pressed her legs together to keep the foetus from escaping her womb. If the last breaths of life hadn't trembled out of her like a half-drowned man reemerging from a lake, she wouldn't have stopped.

Ayu only gave birth (or rather, expelled the foetus from her womb) after her still-warm body, beads of sweat adamantly clinging to her forehead post-exertion, was interred into the cold ground. She was alone when this happened, the prayerful bereaved and gravediggers having left a while ago, but she didn't mind. It was better to carry out this shameful thing, a circumstance all the more hateful because she had no say in it, on her own, than to be accompanied by not only her family and neighbours, but also the admonishments they had in store for her. If I didn't die the way I just did, Ayu's soul thought sarcastically, I probably would've died from hearing what they'd have to say about me.

As she left her body behind, Ayu saw that the baby was a stillborn. Although she hated every second she spent pregnant with it, Ayu couldn't help thinking about how unlucky the poor little bastard was. Being a rape baby was an existence beyond miserable, sure, but didn't it at least deserve a fighting chance, the opportunity to look at shapes in the clouds and breathe in the scent of roadside flowers, and, if nothing else, feel the warmth of its mother's arms?

(She shrank at the last thought.) The longer she considered it, the more Ayu felt a small tinge of guilt crawl all over her like a centipede. If she hadn't held it in, could the baby have lived? Did this make her— she could barely bring herself to think this all the way through—a murderer?

She forced the concept so far back into the recesses of her mind that one couldn't be sure the area it now dwelled in even existed. Not an unfamiliar action: it felt just like forcing the baby's head back down earlier. Nothing could be allowed to interfere with Ayu's conviction in her plan. Besides, its chances for a life worth living were stolen the day it was conceived. The foetus's death was just one of God's kind cruelties.

Ayu felt like a new woman as her spirit floated up and up, leaving behind first an ever-shrinking Earth and then ever-shrinking stars. For the first time in years, she was happy. Her beaten, broken and strained body, and the troubles and suffering she endured like a punishment were down there and she was up here, approaching heights only angels could comprehend. She kept ascending until she stopped at a place filled with nothing but a glowing light that was both blinding and soft. This gleam wasn't the sun—there was some unnamable essence in it, some aspect that hinted at a supernatural quality.

She began trembling as if she were a malnourished child. Ayu felt so weak that she was almost convinced the wind would blot out her very existence, and send it away scattered, like so many fine grains of sand.

"Ayu."

She couldn't pinpoint the source of this voice. It reverberated at an equal volume from all angles, and its owner was nowhere to be seen. Ayu didn't need to see to know who it was though.

"G-God?" She was suddenly filled with a shame born of inadequacy.

"Throughout your life," He boomed, "you have been a good and faithful servant. But like all the others, virtuous and evil, you must wait here until the Judgement Day. It is then that you will know your fate." Ayu wanted to say something, but she wasn't given the opportunity to even move her lips. "Yet I also know this is not what you intended. What is about to happen has nothing to do with My works, but is only the natural result of what you have willed."

That was how she found herself standing off to the side of a brothel in a dimly lit corner of Jakarta. It wasn't one of those classy ones that looked like shiny city-centre hotels—this was a squat grey building with barely a garish neon light to its name. Looking for an opening in the long white dress that had replaced her burial shroud, Ayu's hand slipped under her curtain of black hair and groped all over her back. When she felt the moist squish of her exposed inner organs, she knew her plan had worked.

Ayu was a *sundel bolong* now, the ghost of a woman who died while pregnant out of wedlock.

Someone she knew walked into the brothel. She expected this, of course: all sleazy men, no matter who they were, hung around in the same places. It was simply a law of nature.

※

It all began with her father. On a cool, lazy day—a weekend, if she recalled correctly, something she would rather not do—Ayu sat on his knee while he bounced her lightly. Everything was quite mundane until she felt his hand slip from the small of her back to her butt.

"You know I love you, sweetheart?"

"Yes..." she answered, trying not to sound confused. It wasn't like him to say something like that—not because he was a cold man, but because he, like many other Indonesian parents, simply felt it didn't need to be said.

"And that I'd never do anything to hurt you?"

She nodded in the slow, faint way of someone wanting to speed a conversation along, a nod as indistinct as the fact that he wasn't telling the truth.

What her father did from that day onwards seemed to have opened the floodgates, giving every man in her vicinity and his brother permission to do the same. Schoolteachers who made her stay in for grievous infractions like talking during class, passersby who stole glances at her newly pubescent body, towering seniors, religion teachers too eager to sit close to her during Quran recitation lessons: they all queued in the bread line for a piece, eyes bulging and lips moist like lions strutting around in the butcher shop.

What Ayu never understood was how people perceived this kind of thing. When she, at eight years old, mentioned her father rubbing her thigh in a short essay about the things her parents did to show their love and asked her friend during lunch if her father sometimes grabbed her butt too, her teacher wanted to see her outside of class for obscene talk. There was also that time her parents were summoned by the head of their neighbourhood for "disturbing the public order" because the neighbours had latched onto whisperings about her father's actions. He had to sign a paper promising not to repeat his mistakes, and they never heard anything from Ayu's family again. The neighbours were so happy afterwards, as if they had done something. Satisfied like someone borrowing money to pay off a debt.

Yet as she grew older, the outward displays of disgust and disapproval disappeared. What merited intervention when she was a child, even if it was half-hearted, was now met with a shrug and a wave of the hand at best, and an accusatory *Well, what were you wearing? How did you act around him?* at worst. So was it normal or not? Ayu wondered. How did they determine the cut-off years between abhorrent and expected?

"Men are like beasts," her crumpled black-and-white photograph of a mother said. "They have...a drive, a drive that makes them curious about certain things. This drive can be controlled by education and morals, but it'll never completely go away. All men have demons inside them, Ayu; that's why you can never trust them too much."

These words rang in her mind shortly after what happened with her boyfriend. Although she didn't like to admit it, not even to herself; Ayu knew that agreeing to meet him in a hotel room wasn't going to be a good look for her. But he wasn't that type of man, she thought. He wouldn't force her to do anything. A police officer, dutiful son and deeply religious: he wasn't the type of man that would force his desires on her.

Yet plenty of police officers, dutiful sons and deeply religious men had forced themselves on her for years now, and he was determined to join these ranks, entrench himself into this hall of fame.

✳

She knew that, for her boyfriend, time wasn't reduced to a meaningless, nonexistent slurry after the rape. She also knew he didn't feel, from that point on, like a dead person walking or a restless ghost, even after her anonymous vent on a forum site became as viral as an epidemic. Why would he? As a police officer, he was above the law. And more than that, it didn't change anything about him. He could move along and chase a career and wander the world over or do anything else young men did without his actions becoming for him a ball and chain around his ankle. But Ayu couldn't do anything about what he carelessly put inside her, this thing that moulded her body to tell everyone what had happened that night.

Ayu didn't stay around to see the outrage her story elicited online after it went viral on Twitter, or how he was arrested and jailed as a result of this. Not that it would've made any difference: sympathy and a verdict that came too late wouldn't have un-raped her or taken away the bag of stones in her womb.

✳

So men all have demons inside them, do they? She thought. Well, I'll be a demon to scatter all of theirs to hell.

Ayu walked slowly, with a swish to her hips. The man couldn't help but look. Of course he couldn't— this *was* the senior she'd caught taking pictures up her skirt when she was fifteen.

"*Mas*," she crooned, "don't you think you deserve more than those whores? You're better off spending the night with me. I'm a virgin." Her lips tightened into a sweet smile.

There was an odd and almost impossible mix of fear and enticement on his face. She looked like the girls from the hentais he watched or one of those biracial actresses that dominated the country's movie screens. But they weren't the type to be out this late, were they?

Without his knowing it, his legs sent him following her with an intensity that almost had him floating in mid-air.

They escaped the city's glaring eyes in an alleyway, together amongst the overflowing bins and rats and a persistent smell of decay. He trembled and switched between tentatively reaching out his hand and pulling it away, not daring to make eye contact for a single second.

"Come on," she breathed out, "don't be shy." Ayu stepped forward and embraced him, letting the man's head lay on her chest.

This shot into his veins a boldness previously missing, but that didn't help him take off Ayu's gown before she shredded him into a mess of dead flesh and blood.

She lured the others with the ease of a bird flying in a clear summer sky. It didn't require much finesse, since their half-stupid, horny brains did most of the work for her. All Ayu had to do was walk and stand around in a way that showed off her curves, and promise them an encounter in a sultry, breathy voice that disgusted her every time she heard herself use it. They would've trudged all seven continents for her then, let alone some dark, grotty little pocket of the city where nothing good could ever happen. The easiness of it all made Ayu yawn.

As she made her way through Jakarta and its suburbs, Ayu noticed that women would clutch their babies tighter when they saw her, and thought them needlessly prejudiced. She wasn't like the other *sundel bolongs* who prowled in the night for babies as well as men—truth be told, she'd had enough of them for more than a lifetime. Besides, there was no satisfaction for her in eating a baby compared to draining the blood of a woman, like for instance, her mother.

After doing away with most of the brothel's customer base—a job that surprised her because, experienced as she was with the ways of seedy men, she didn't expect to recognise so many faces—Ayu made her way to a nearby jail. Despite the justice system being as corrupt as a malware-infected computer, she still indulged in the idealistic belief that they had to have locked up a *rapist* at some point, especially one that brought so much shame to the institution of policing.

Her ex wasn't in any of the cells.

She checked the other prisons nearby. He wasn't in any of them either. Chastising herself for being so naive, Ayu paid a visit to his house.

It was no different than the other unpainted, one-storey houses in the neighbourhood, except for its interior. The modesty of furniture and ambience Ayu was accustomed to had been overtaken by newly polished tables, plumped-up chairs and amplified lighting, unusually bright as if to greet some new hope. When she entered the dining room, she saw him, his parents, a woman around her age and another middle-aged couple who must have been her parents sitting around the table. They were too preoccupied with their jovial discussion of marriage and wedding plans to notice her.

She was much harder to ignore when she pulled her ex away, castrated him and tossed the limp and bloody ragdoll away. No longer interested in that mass of leftovers, she edged closer and closer towards his and the woman's family, pushing them into a corner as they stumbled out of their chairs.

"W-We never did anything to you!" his fiancée stammered. "Please, leave us alone!"

His mother was on the verge of crying. "You can see there are two men left," she said, not caring that her husband and the woman's father could hear.

"Have them! Why would a *sundel bolong* like you want anything to do with us women?"

The question lingered in the air unanswered, mixing with the stench of blood and death.

＊

Ayu didn't alter her form when she paid a visit home. Her father was on the edge of a heart attack when he saw her, his pale face unchangeably frozen in its gape-mouthed expression after she was done with him.

"Darling, please," her mother said, backing away while still in bed, "I tried to protect you, I asked him to stop. You wouldn't hurt your own mother, would you?"

"Tried?" Ayu replied. "I needed more than that!" There was a faint, near-crying tremble to her thundering yell as though a hurt child had taken hold of her voice.

While staring down at the bodies of her parents and pondering everything she had done that night, Ayu realised she didn't feel any satisfaction at all: rather, there arose within her a vague sense of having neglected to do something crucial. As she wondered why this was so, Ayu's mind drifted to how her experiences were not at all unique.

Every girl she befriended in her youth and every woman she had met or heard of seemed to have at least one story to tell about being touched, groped, gawked at, wolf-whistled, cat-called, photographed without consent, harassed through text or raped. It was strange, really, since disgust for these acts was supposedly universal. What was more, all of those women and girls seemed to have also, at some point, come up against another woman unflinchingly determined to protect their man or boy from the slightest consequences for his actions, regardless of how well they knew (and there could be no doubt they knew).

The idea struck her with its lightning, and Ayu instantly knew what she had to do.

Over the course of that night and the next day, Ayu gutted every house, school, prison, government building, *pesantren*, police station, court of law, office, nightclub, mosque, factory, church, street, alleyway, brothel, hotel room, bus, train, taxi and rideshare in the country. Towns that would've been left without men by any other *sundel bolong* were now nearly empty of either sex. As she gazed at what she had made of a newly bloodied classroom, Ayu began floating involuntarily.

She was back in that endless glowing space in minutes, her flowing black hair and stained white gown replaced by the hairstyle and clothes she wore when she died. That feeling of lightness was back again.

Ayu tried imagining angels opening the gates of Heaven for her. In this scenario, she would saunter around, her step light as if she never lived her kind of life, and see for herself the sumptuous feasts, lush gardens, glittering mansions and clear, cool springs of paradise. It all seemed so beautiful: the pearls, the golden thrones, the jewels and carpets and cushions and silk. In her yearning for these sights and sensations, she couldn't help but wonder if, after all she had done, God would still save a spot for her. Fearing blasphemy, Ayu tried to ignore how she didn't consider these prospects totally fulfilling. She wondered if it was possible to ask God to send her the other way, hoping that unfinished business with its future inhabitants would be justification enough.

iishch'id

Perfect Immortality

River Eno

We met on Halloween, on a jack-o-lantern lit street in my hometown, illuminated by October's full Hunter moon. He was dressed as a vampire with white makeup, fake fangs and an accent I'd never heard before. I figured he was from the posh side of town. I was sixteen and dressed as a witch with old scraps from my mother's closet and a drug store pointy hat. He said I was perfect.

✳

When I turned eighteen, he paid to have my eye color changed. It was all the rage. He assured me my brown eyes were beautiful, but green would set off my perfect red hair. He said the procedure would be quick and painless, but it took a long while for my dark eyes to lighten, and the clamps left deep bruises. The dryness and blurred vision followed me for weeks. And that's when the headaches started.

My mother was beside herself. She said I looked cold and vacant, alien, not the daughter she recognized. She droned on about "men like him." Callous older men who used young girls, changing them into what they wanted and then throwing them away. She said he was emotionless, and he'd expect a lot more from me after shelling out so much money. She always said mean things about men after my dad left. But he said he had to get away from this crap town, that it was killing him. He used to write to me about the cities he stayed in. I wish he'd taken me with him.

I couldn't listen to her insist I wasn't pretty anymore, so I packed my clothes, grabbed the stuffed owl my dad left me and moved out.

✳

At twenty-one he paid for breast augmentation surgery. That's what the doctor called it. He said he loved my slimmer, more athletic body, but the blouses he bought me needed to be filled out. I was bedridden for almost a month, an allergy to the pain medication.

My mother harped on me when I'd visit, lamenting the daughter she'd had, comparing the things I used to do—working at the library, seeing friends at the lake and sunbathing—to the new me, his girlfriend. Her yelling made the headaches worse. I wanted her to love me as I was, but she made a big deal out of every single thing. She said she saw the beautiful part of me that I'd see when I was older. I didn't know what that meant.

He said I was perfect.

✳

For my twenty-fifth birthday he threw a Halloween masquerade in the elegant gardens at his country home. He told me I was a full-grown woman. He hired an Austrian make-up artist to highlight my perfect features. Before the party he told me not to speak unless spoken to and to always keep my answers brief. He had a white silk dress made for me, to show off my perfect body.

The guests wore white gowns, black tuxedos, and ornate Carnivale masks. I was formally introduced to everyone, over one hundred strangers. They curtsied and kissed my hand while he stood behind me, tightening his fingers around my arm if I said more than, thank you. He always made sure I didn't make a fool of myself.

At precisely three in the morning, bathed in the light of the full moon, he took me to the dais in the middle of the grounds, had me bow to his guests and then sank his teeth deep into my neck, ripping into my carotid artery and letting me bleed out on the grass. He told me to beg him to save me with his blood…so I did.

✳

When I woke, I marveled how the strength of my new body made it look graceful and flawless. The dull headache that plagued me since the eye surgery was gone. He gave me new clothes and told me I had to say a proper goodbye to my mother before we left for his estate in Dresden. He said I would feel regret and guilt if I didn't have closure, and he wanted our life to be perfectly free of any constraints.

Mom got hysterical when she saw me. Was nearly inconsolable when I told her I was leaving the country with him. Nine years and she was still bitter that I had love and hers had left. I was glad I was leaving, and I told her so.

*

Learning another country's customs was easier with his guidance, however temperamental he may have been when giving it. Many moons passed, situating my old life five decades behind me. And it was a perfect life...when he was pleased, which didn't seem to be often as of late...or I don't know, maybe ever. No matter how much I learned I never did the right thing in front of the right people. I began to cherish the moments he left me alone. It was the only time I was sure not to disappoint him.

He told me he was throwing a masquerade for the Hunter Moon falling on Samhain. The first such ball since my bloody rebirth. I was excited to wear a costume like I'd seen at the first masquerade. He laughed, and said the dress he wanted me to wear would arrive the next day.

*

I spent a lot of time in the attic of his family's vast mountain manse, filled with centuries-old furniture and art. He'd shown me the old masquerade costumes, years ago, packed away. The large crate made of cedar, the lid hinged with medieval hardware and the gowns stored in strange paper, one atop the other.

I chose a black gown with real emerald accents and took it to the large floor mirror by the window. I held the dress up admiring the moonlight twinkling off the jewels, deciding how to tell him this was my choice when I noticed a plastic container next to a cloth covered bureau.

I knew what it was—modern in a sea of ancient— the container I'd packed when I left home. I hadn't seen it in a very long time, and I couldn't remember how it got to the attic. I opened it as if it wasn't mine, as if the girl from back then wasn't me. But inside were my clothes, if from another life. My snowy owl, now old and gray. I touched it gently. My memory was sharp...when had I packed it away? Had I put it up here?

I found a small box still wrapped in shipping paper, my mother's name in the return address, written in her hand. I didn't remember receiving it. A small card was tucked inside.

"A collection of memories to tether us through time."

A sweet message as she could be on occasion. I was suddenly afraid. I rarely thought of my life before the change, and not since I learned she'd passed on.

A small album sat on top, photos of me when I was a baby. The classic ones, on the belly with my head held high, then sitting up with my big brown eyes wide. My eyes had been brown…I looked in the mirror. The pale green orbs were shocking compared to the warmth of the picture.

The next photo was when my mother and I were at the beach. I was lanky, my smile bright, and my long, red hair hung in corkscrews. I remembered mom snapping the picture and suddenly felt the ghost of her through the picture's point of view, seeing myself through her eyes. I heard her voice lamenting how beautiful and vibrant I was before the changes.

I fingered through the jewelry, my Grams diamond pin, my high school ring. I stared at the pictures for some time, hearing myself yell at her, tell her I was glad to be leaving, to be rid of her. I looked at the dirty, gray owl. A tangible testament of my father's abandonment.

Pain assaulted my chest and tears sprang to my eyes. A fierce longing for who I was completely enveloped me. How could I have left her that way...alone?

✳

I charged from the attic and found him in the study. I set the photo album and shipping paper on his desk.

"Why didn't you ever give this to me?" I asked quietly, my voice shaking with rage and sadness and fear.

He stared back, taking a breath as he does when I anger him. "I thought it best not to upset you."

"You said...the way I was...you said I was perfect."

"I knew you could be." He smirked, his dark blue eyes unblinking, challenging. When I didn't move, he stood. "Wear this to the ball tomorrow evening." He handed me a hanger holding a plain black dress and left the room.

The ache in my chest grew heavier. I was as my mother said...an object he molded to his perfection.

✳

Being All Hallow's Eve, the ball was in the family graveyard. He didn't seem to mind party goers

140

walking over his long departed. The costumes were more stunning than the first masquerade, and more contrived, the painfully bored trying to be relevant. The women wore blood red suits with lavish black eye masks. The men, black gowns with red half-masks.

They complimented me and smiled as if we were friends, but I wasn't allowed friends. The basic black dress he made me wear was embarrassing, a nightgown next to the opulence of the masqueraders. The longer I stood with him, the more resentment rose within me. I didn't care if he put a diamond crown on my head if it meant I had to give up another piece of myself.

At precisely 3am, he guided me to the large fountain in the middle of the extravagant gardens, holding my arm to maneuver me around the headstones. Two fully masked men carried a sleek black coffin from the brushwood. They set it twenty feet from the fountain and in front of the guests. He took a step forward, toward the coffin. The revelers became still. He had me bow.

"Step in, my beloved." He smiled as the coffin lid was opened by the two men who carried it out.

"What?"

He waved his hand toward the coffin. "Step in, my beloved," he repeated.

"No."

The word popped out but was uneasy. Whispers fluttered through the silence. I looked at the coffin and then at him.

"No."

"Step in, my beloved," he repeated, sharper.

Instinct moved me away from him, toward the fountain. His expression turned cold.

"Come now…" He seized my arm with unearthly strength and speed. "Do you not want this to be perfect?"

He pulled so hard, I stumbled into the fountain, my hands knocking into staves of wood stacked on the ledge. He swore under his breath in German, grabbed one of the staves, then yanked me upright to face the crowd. He sternly set me in my place by the coffin before stepping toward the guests.

"Good evening," he said, with a tight smile. "Forgive my perfect bride, she's not been herself…the last few years."

Everyone laughed. His smile relaxed and widened to the beautiful expression I had, at one time, cherished. The smile I believed told the truth. I was so wrong. I had never been safe. He was insidious and threatening. And my mother had seen right through it.

"To continue," he said, holding up the wood with one hand to regain everyone's attention. "Thank you all for coming, and please indulge me in a trip down memory lane."

He began the story of how we met.

"She wore a dollar store hat atop her wild flaming hair. She was beautiful, yet not quite perfect."

A recounting that used to fill me with pride made me sick. Entertainment was all I was. I glanced around the family cemetery filled with desiccated loved ones.

Then at the coffin.

Finally at him holding the spike of wood in his hand as he prattled on about our lives together.

Entertainment was all I ever was…to my last breath.

My fingers tightened into a fist. But I had always been the perfect pupil. I listened. I learned. Heated emotions, like anger and desire, were to be harnessed. Patience embraced.

"Even after having left her mortal life behind," he continued, "she could be rough around the edges."

The crowd snickered. He laughed with them. The stake in his hand.

Know your opportunity.

His other hand reached back for me as he spoke.

Seize the moment.

I moved toward him. Wrapped my fingers around his wrist with one hand and snatched the stake from his grip with the other. I was fast. He was shocked. I jammed that splinter of wood into his back. And pushed until it burst through his chest.

Snickers turned to a collective gasp. With my hands still gripped around the bloody stake, I pointed him toward the open coffin. I let go, and he collapsed face first into the white satin sheets. His lower legs in the air, resting against the coffin's edge.

I will never again be entertainment.

The mass of menacingly anonymous onlookers approached, and I moved back.

An older woman, tall, in a black lace suit, bejeweled and feathered mask came from the crowd toward me. She looked at him. She looked at me.

"He was going to kill me," I said, my voice shaking.

"Yes." She smiled. She bent to one knee, and the rest of the masqueraders followed.

It took me a moment to catch up, looking over the sea of masked people genuflecting as he lay hemorrhaging in the coffin meant for me. His empire was mine now.

"We've seen his show dozens of times. But this…this was the best ending, My Queen."

I straightened and had to agree.

This was perfect.

zǐ gōng

Famine

Sydney Hodges

Dawn finds you in your bed, wide-eyed, starving, trying to hold yourself together.

While your heart drums a raucous beat, you're not afraid--haven't been for a while now. It makes you wonder if all that deferred fear will come rushing in at the end.

The end.

There's a finality to every heartbeat that has much to do with the void in your stomach. It's been weeks, and not so much as a crumb has passed your lips and stayed there. Scattered on your kitchen counters are ashen chocolate bars, a plate with a slice of molding brambleberry pie, a bowl of oatmeal that's seen better days, a Granny Smith apple, a white nectarine, a Bartlett pear all in various stages of oxidation and decay. Every one of them with a single, crescent bite removed.

There's the coppery sunlight creeping through your window, dim and enervated through the smog. Its muted beams have always reminded you of an alien planet nudged a little too far from its sun. Maybe things would've been easier had you actually been an extraterrestrial. This world has never made you feel "human," and it would've been less painful to bear if it'd all been your fault.

You delicately clear a lock of hair from your face. It comes away in your fingers. You're not afraid, but your blood knows something's coming.

Circling a drain, spiraling tighter and tighter before falling into the dark.

A shudder rolls across the plains of your bare skin as you try with all your might to keep the hunger from tearing you apart. You'd cried at first, trying to keep more than a morsel from exploding from behind your teeth. Your old ways--meditating, counting, breathing, eating food--aren't going to cut it. There's no safe harbor in the storm within you.

You were seven when you first felt the storm brewing. It was easier back then because children have always been hungry, reaching creatures. The only clean bowls were on the top shelf, pushed all the way to the back. You stood on your toes and gasped when your arm reached up, up, *up* past the bare, dusty shelves, to the very top, your elongated, spindly fingers brushing against ceramic a full four feet above you. Your guardians looked at you funny when they saw you devouring Frosted Flakes from their nice Mediterranean salad bowl, but they never asked how you managed to reach it. They didn't look at you funny anymore because they stopped looking at you altogether.

That same year, you and a hundred of your peers were at an assembly applauding one overachiever after another. Your claps began to ring hollow, and your hands felt strange...tight. You looked down at your fingers. They'd fused into mitts, not threadbare like your actual mittens, but fully fleshed. A scream hand-cranked its way up your throat, but before you could let it out and guarantee humiliation for years after this, your hands returned to normal--five little fingers on each hand, ready to clap for the Honor Roll recipients.

One morning, you woke up with the top half of your stuffed rabbit sticking out of your chest, its ears meshed with your forearms. The rest of it tickled your lungs. None of it caused you pain--what hurt was keeping the scream bottled up so you wouldn't disturb your guardians. An hour passed while you extricated Bun-Bun from your flesh, the baby-soft skin of your cheeks drinking up hot tears. When it was finally over, Bun-Bun went straight into the garbage.

You learned to eat alone lest anyone see the way you now ate. You avoided sports in high school, not that you were good at them anyway. And that was easy--all it took was your clavicle erupting out of you like a calcified wing during the softball unit.

Everyone left you alone after that. The stares were the worst part. Your classmates didn't even hate you--the fear in their eyes did more to convince you that you were a monster than words ever could.

Things only got more complicated as you grew, even as you learned to contain yourself better. Like many people, you spent your twenties searching for what would satiate you--pain, pleasure, you were a pendulum that swung between both. Never felt like you had enough. Those who spent time with you, on the other hand, would leave your dorm full to bursting, having gotten what they wanted, nothing more, nothing less. You sustained them with what amounted to a grain of sand, compared to all that you had to give, while they offered nothing. Nothing but the fear that if they fed you crumbs, you'd come back, flapping and squawking for more.

It's too much, they'd say. *Like there's a famine in you.*

One of them, a sweet one, described you as "all-consuming" on your first night together, earnest lips trembling with adoration. The second time it was uttered, it was their voice that quavered just before the door closed between the two of you forever. Shame soaked you down to your bones, which back then fidgeted constantly beneath your muscles, restless and ignorant of your need to avoid scrutiny.

Not all met you with terror. There were those who experienced you as a dream. They'd tell you their fantasies while smiling into your hair or brushing your collarbone with sighs wistful for a different reality.

You'd watch their tongues shine and dance with tales of how you reached deep into them and retrieved their hearts, devouring them as a god would ambrosia. In the reverence that silked their whispered confessions and polished their eyes was a wish made clear: that they might watch as you rent them so beautifully and clap at the sight of their own destruction.

And there were those who played similar images behind their eyelids, only they called them nightmares. Their mouths grew small with the instinct of prey as they minced out how you tore out their hearts and peeled away slivers with a black, demonic light in your eyes. As if speaking it aloud would invoke it. Their voices at once held awe and despair, and their skin prickled with an unspoken dread: that you might have them watch while you obliterated them, their hollow chests steaming and heaving.

There was a heady power in the mundane. It made you feel human to soothe the dreamers' needs with an indulgent kiss, to reassure the fearful with a caress too soft, too gentle, for a heart-eater to give. But there was a part of you that yearned to carry out the will of your dreamers and to embody the very thing that made your anxious lovers tremble. It wasn't that you believed yourself incapable. It was that, once you started, you didn't think you could stop. You could never allow yourself to let a hand sink into a lover's rib cage and grasp that beating muscle--*the best part of them*--in your hand, then between your teeth.

What you did allow posed less danger. You took your dreamers by the hand and let them glimpse the real you as their hands melded with yours. You brought one of them close to the quivering muscle beneath ever-shifting bone. Your limbs stretched farther than you ever thought flesh and bone could accommodate, your skin millimeter-thin. You joined your bones with theirs, muscles twitching in rapture as they fused, and neither of you cared whether there was an undo button.

A blink, and the attenuated sunlight is on its last legs, casting the room in sickly persimmon. While everything on the wrong side of your skin sits stale and dim, your ribcage swells with the roiling squall inside you, then cracks, the sound of crashing waves and rumbling thunder leaving your mouth. All that you have held back--the sheer force of your power, the wrath tamped down like bitter espresso grounds--it all spills out of you, *you* spill out of you until there's nothing left but your heart turned inside out and blown out to five times its size.

This world may not welcome what emerges. Something sighs within you:

The world has always feared what doesn't serve it.

A strange fullness beneath your sternum builds to diastolic ecstasy as your next breath sends tears burning down your cheeks.

It's holding the last sweet, heady sip of wine in your mouth just before it goes down smooth, isn't it?

A shiver ripples from your freshly skinned heart outward, an epicenter of something delicious and unsilenceable. When it ends, your body is lighter, uncluttered, and unburdened enough to give your soul room to grow.

And feast.

You still don't know what you are, but you know you won't go hungry any longer.

So many in your life snatched you with their greedy hands and placed you on their tongues like a holy wafer, only to spit you out when they realized it was a bite of decadent cake. They never wanted the richness within you, only what you could do for them.

As for those savory lovers who begged you to rend their muscle and bones between your teeth-- your blood sizzles at the knowledge that they understood you better than anyone. At last able to fulfill their wishes, you will spare them from the end of everything.

Your maw opens wide enough now to swallow them whole. They will dwell within you for the rest of eternity, both of you finally sated.

Dusk finds you in your true form, ready to bring famine to the world by ending your own, each cloven step drumming the ground to the beat of your own gospel.

And it's only the beginning.

Acknowledgements

Her name was Jina, but the authorities identify her by her Persian name, Mahsa Amini. She was reserved, easy going, disinterested in politics, although she wanted to be a lawyer. She was from a small town, visiting the capital city with her family to see her uncle.

And she died because of her clothes.

Some reports say she didn't wear a hijab. Some say she was wearing pants that were too tight. Some say her hijab was too loose, or worn incorrectly. Her mother claims all of that is untrue and her daughter was dressed in accordance to the laws. Regardless, the morality police ignored Jina's pleas and her brother's explanation that they were not from the area. They grabbed her and forced her into a van.

The other women detained in that van say she was insulted, taunted, that she cried and pleaded to be let go, to be given a chance to correct the problem. That she didn't know or understand. That she was so afraid.

And then the "morality police" hit her. In the head. Over and over.

By the time she reached the detention center, she was losing consciousness.

By the time they got her to the hospital, she was in a coma.

And then they lied.

They lied because it's not the first time this has happened, and because they've always gotten away with it before.

They lied because they could.

When Jina died, on September 16, they blamed her and her family, and they denied any responsibility.

She was twenty-two.

She wanted to grow up, to get a college education. To get married and have a family.

She just wanted the chance to live a happy life.

We acknowledge Jina.

We acknowledge that women have been blamed for their own beatings, their own rapes, their own murders for far too long.

We acknowledge that this world will use any excuse to ignore our cries for justice. To close its eyes to what it has done to us. That women of color receive the worst of this ignorance and brutality.

We acknowledge that too many women are sacrificed to teach the men in power that we bleed, that we scream, that we are real, thinking, feeling flesh and blood humans. That even when we are broken, we are called liars, overreactors, trouble makers.

Weak.

Jina was twenty-two. She wasn't interested in politics. She just wanted a simple, happy life.

And she died because a group of men didn't like the look of her.

Women are groomed from birth to appease the fragile rage of men. To smile and pander and dress correctly to avoid our own rapes and murders.

If we survive, we are told all the ways we failed.

We acknowledge the struggle of women and gender minorities. We acknowledge the struggle of women of color.

We acknowledge the danger we live in every single day.

But we must also acknowledge that there are more of us than there are of them.

We acknowledge that we've been told where to go, what to wear, what not to say, what not to do to be good girls. To not be murdered.

We acknowledge that these rules have never protected us.

We acknowledge Jina, and the brave women of Iran who are fighting every day for the right not to be killed for their clothes.

We do not have to live like this anymore.

We acknowledge our power.

We're coming.

ABOUT THE AUTHORS

LCW Allingham is a shit starter with a big mouth. Sometimes she writes stuff.

River Eno Vegan, Pagan, Editor, studying herbalism. Author of Urban Fantasy *The Anastasia Evolution Series*. Her corporeal shell resides on the East Coast in one reality while her brain travels to alternate realities daily.

A.R.C. Mitra writes gothic horror, ghost stories and retold fairy tales and folklore. Originally from California, she spent years living in New Zealand and is currently based in New York City. She holds degrees in English, History and Law. Her work has recently been published in *Dark Moon Digest*. She enjoys writing at 2am in the morning, video-calling her mother's cats and the smell of old books.

Dale W. Glaser is a lifelong collector, re-teller and occasional inventor of fantasy tales. He has published over 40 short stories, plus various pieces of poetry, drabble and flash fiction. He needs air, food, water and stories in order to survive, not necessarily in that order. His lifelong love of written words has manifested as a devotion to the English language almost exclusively, which is probably just as well because if he were to master any of the dead tongues that conceal ancient mysteries and invoke malevolent forces, we'd all be in trouble. He currently lives in Virginia with his wife, their three children, and a rotating roster of pets. Six to eight is a good estimate of how many animals cohabit with the family at any given time.

Sydney Hodges spent her formative years bouncing between the East and West Coasts as a military brat. This made for a memorable childhood, during which she picked up hobbies like collecting bones and shed snakeskin in the Nevada desert. Growing up on a steady diet of horror movies gave her the gift of fear as well as a deep appreciation for monsters and the supernatural, which inform much of her writing today. Sydney is currently a gamer and emerging writer living in Washington, D.C. with her wonderful significant other and their sweet dog, Stella, who often comforts her during scary movies.

Maureen O'Leary lives in California. Her work appears or is forthcoming in Black Spot Books' *Under Her Skin*, Flame Tree Press' *Alternate History*, *The Esopus Reader*, *Passengers Journal*, *Reckon Review*, *Bourbon Penn*, *Penumbric Speculative Fiction*, *Tales To Terrify*, *Occulum*, *Sequestrum*, *Nightmare*, and *Sycamore Review* among others. She is a graduate of Ashland MFA and managing editor of The Black Fork Review.

Sofia Tantono Sofia Tantono is a writer based in Jakarta, Indonesia. Her works have appeared or are forthcoming in *unstamatic*, *Yuwana Zine* and *ārasi*, among others. Outside of her writing, Sofia was the curator of *Yuwana Zine's* fifth issue and is *Koening Zine's* fiction editor.

Hope Madden is a writer, filmmaker and film critic based in Columbus, Ohio. Her poetry and short fiction have appeared in numerous journals including *Wild Good Poetry Review* as well as Z Publishing's *Best Emerging Poets: An Anthology*. Her first feature film, *Obstacle Corpse*, was completed in 2022. Her first novella, *Roost*, also saw its first light in 2022, publishing in March of that year from Off Limits Press.

For more information and links to author websites and social media, visit speculationpub.com/authors

Check out the Collections of Utter Speculation

The Lost Colony of Roanoke
The Jersey Devil
Lady in White
The Dancing Plague

www.speculationpub.com